SUPER GENIUS
SCIENCE QUIZ

Dilip M. Salwi is a Delhi-based science writer. A winner of several national awards and fellowships for popularizing science, he also writes science fiction and plays involving science and scientists. Author of forty-four books, his *The Robots are Coming, 1000 Science Quiz, Meet the Four Elements, The Story of Zero, Chemline Book of Quotable Science, Folk Tales of Science* and *Inventions that Made History* are bestsellers.

SUPER GENIUS
SCIENCE QUIZ

Dilip M. Salwi

RUPA

Published by
Rupa Publications India Pvt. Ltd. 2004
7/16, Ansari Road, Daryaganj
New Delhi 110002

Sales centres:
Allahabad Bengaluru Chennai
Hyderabad Jaipur Kathmandu
Kolkata Mumbai

ISBN: 978-81-716-7179-3

Tenth impression 2018

15 14 13 12 11 10

Hello! Science Quiz Buffs!

More than fifteen years ago, when my publisher suggested I write a science quiz book, I was somewhat reluctant. I had written quiz questions on science for a children's magazine from my college days and so I thought I should do something different. But his persuasion finally won me over, and I sat down to write the book.

At the outset I decided that my book would, despite being a quiz book, give a holistic, total picture of science and technology, including the effects of science on society. In consultation with my friend Dr. N.R. Mankad I thought of having 1000 quiz questions in the book with the hope that it would turn out to be the magical number . And so it has. Published in 1988, it has today gone into more than 18 editions and is still the best-selling quiz book. Subsequently, my publisher brought out a 1000 series of quiz books on other subject. In due couse, some clones of my book also appeared in the market. Who says students are not interested in science?

Naturally, such an old quiz book needs revision and updating as the scientific scenario has changed over the years. I have also split the aforementioned book into two handy parts with more new questions but retaining the holistic flavour of the previous book. In tune with the popular 'Super Quiz' series I brought out recently for kids and children, I have also renamed the two books, 'Super Expert Science Quiz' and 'Super Genius Science

Quiz'. For easy reading of the answers, I have also changed the format. I have also included a scoring board to assess oneself in science awareness. I am sure all these changes will be appreciated by my young readers.

I reiterate here that these books test your 'Science Awareness' and not science as such becasue it is my personal feeling that science cannot be tested by quiz questions. I am sure they will prove as attractive and stimulating to my young readers as the previous book proved to be. If these books sustain my readers' interest in science and technology in these days when it is present in all walks of life, my purpose in writing them will be fulfilled.

Delhi
July 19, 2003

Dilip M. Salwi

Acknowledgements

The following agencies and individuals are to be thanked for the photographs published in the book: Asoka Samanta, U.S.I.S., New Delhi; Ravi Datta, British High Commission, New Delhi; Shankar, French Information Center, New Delhi; German News Agency, New Delhi; Indian Space Research Organisation, Bangalore; Raman Research Institute, Bangalore; World Health Organisation, New Delhi; Bose Institue, Kolkata; Visvesvaraya Industrial Museum of Science and Technology, Bangalore; Dinesh Sinha and P.Dayanandan. And last but not the least, I am thankful to Ajay Gupta for keying the book on the computer and my wife Smriti, daughter Neha and son Romel for bearing patiently with me while I was revising this book.

Dilip M. Salwi

CONTENTS

I

TRAILBLAZERS

Fathers

1. Who is known as the Father of geology?
   - (a) Alfred Wegener
   - (b) Charles Lyell
   - (c) James Hutton
   - (d) Philon

2. Who is the Father of the automobile?
   - (a) Rudolf Diesel
   - (b) Henry Ford
   - (c) Gottlieb Daimler
   - (d) Carl Benz

3. Who is the Father of the Periodic Table of Elements?
   - (a) Alfred Nobel
   - (b) Dimitri Mendeleev
   - (c) Johann Baeyer
   - (d) Johannes Van der Waals

4. Who is the Father of the science of chemotherapy. i.e., using chemicals to treat diseases?
    (a) Robert Koch
    (b) Emil Behring
    (c) Paul Ehrlich
    (d) Louis Pasteur

5. Who is considered to be the Father of Cybernetics?
    (a) Claude Shannon
    (b) Konrad Zuse
    (c) Norbert Wiener
    (c) Alan Turing

6. Who is the Father of the hydrogen bomb?
    (a) J. Robert Oppenheimer
    (b) Leo Szilard
    (c) Edward Teller
    (d) Otto Hahn

7. Who is considered to be the Father of plastic surgery?
    (a) Hippocrates
    (b) Galen
    (c) Susruta
    (d) Charaka

8. Who is considered to be the Father of brain surgery?
    (a) Pierre Broca
    (b) Galen
    (c) Harvey Cushing
    (c) Christian Barnard

9. Who is the Father of geology in India?
    (a) Mihir Sen
    (b) D. N. Wadia
    (c) K. S. Valdiya
    (d) M. K. Bose

10. Which mathematician is considered to be the Father of the philosophy of infinity?
    - (a) Bhaskara
    - (b) Leonard Euler
    - (c) Zeno
    - (d) Euclid

11. Who the Father of physiology?
    - (a) Erasistratus
    - (b) Thales
    - (c) Anaximander
    - (d) Herophilus

12. Who is the founding Father of modern anatomy?
    - (a) James Y. Simpson
    - (b) Andreas Vesalius
    - (c) Hippocrates
    - (d) Avicenna

13. Who is considered to be the Father of eugenics?
    - (a) Karl Pearson
    - (b) Charles Davenport
    - (c) Francis Galton
    - (d) Charles Darwin

Discoverers

14. Who discovered the Third Law of Thermodynamics?
    - (a) Count Rumford
    - (b) L.E. Boltzmann
    - (c) P.M.S. Blackett
    - (d) H.W. Nernst

15. Who discovered artificial radioactivity?
    - (a) Henri Bacquerel
    - (b) Pierre Curie
    - (c) Marie Curie
    - (d) Frederic Joliot-Curie

16. Who discovered sulpha drugs?
    (a) Howard Florey   (b) Gerhard Domagk
    (c) Alexander Fleming (d) Robert Wilkins

17. The 'primitive' portion of the human brain is known after a medical man who discovered it. Who is he?
    (a) A R. Wallace   (b) Pierre Broca
    (c) Paul Bert   (d) W.C. Gorgas

18. Who discovered the fact that fish wear 'war paint' to indicate their territories?
    (a) Francis Galton   (b) B. F. Skinner
    (c) Karl von Frisch   (d) Konrad Lorenz

19. Who discovered radioactivity?
    (a) Pierre Curie   (b) Wilhelm Roentgen
    (c) John Rayleigh   (d) Henri Becquerel

20. Who discovered the Ionisation formula, which is considered to be one of the ten major discoveries in astrophysics?
    (a) Norman Lockyer   (b) Carl Sagan
    (c) M.N. Saha   (d) Edwin Hubble

21. Like Isaac Newton, who independently discovered calculus?
    (a) G.W. Leibniz   (b) Christian Huygens
    (c) Francis Bacon   (d) Leonardo Fibonacci

22. Who discovered one-celled animals?
    - (a) Marcello Malpighi
    - (b) Anton Leeuwenhoek
    - (c) Charaka
    - (d) Galen

23. Who discovered J–receptor–the nerve terminals in lungs that cause breathlessness?
    - (a) B. S. Anand
    - (b) Avtar Singh Paintal
    - (c) A. L. Hodgkin
    - (d) Peter Medawar

24. Who discovered that malaria is caused by a particular type of mosquito?
    - (a) Ronald Ross
    - (b) Charles Sherrington
    - (c) Christian Eijkman
    - (d) Louis Pasteur

25. Who discovered 'imprinting'?
    - (a) Charles Darwin
    - (b) B. F. Skinner
    - (c) Konrad Lorenz
    - (d) Alfred Russel Wallace

26. Who discovered that honeybees transmit information about the direction and distance of nectar-rich flowers by their humming dance?
    - (a) Niko Tinbergen
    - (b) I. P. Pavlov
    - (c) Karl R. von Frisch
    - (d) Stephen Jay Gould

27. Who discovered 'conditioned reflex' through his experiments on dogs?
    - (a) I. P. Pavlov
    - (b) B. F. Skinner
    - (c) Sigmund Freud
    - (d) Carl Jung

28. Who discovered ionosphere, the electrically charged layer surrounding the earth, that makes radio communication possible?
    (a) Robert Watson-Watt (b) E.V. Appleton
    (c) J.J. Thomson   (d) J. D. Cockcroft

29. Who discovered radio waves coming from the sky?
    (a) Max Weber   (b) J.S. Hey
    (c) Karl Jansky   (d) Robert Watson-Watt

Propounders

30. Who coined the term 'anaesthesia' for any pain-killer given during an operation?
    (a) Paul Ehrlich
    (b) Susruta
    (c) Oliver Wendell Holmes
    (d) Bertrand Russell

31. Who came close to predicting the presence of black holes?
    (a) S. Chandrasekhar   (b) Albert Einstein
    (c) A. S. Eddington   (d) Harlow Shapley

32. Who introduced the concept of 'Brown dwarfs'– objects in a stage of evolution between planets and stars?
    (a) Shiv Kumar   (b) H.N. Russell
    (c) John Flamsteed   (d) S. Chandrashekhar

33. The comet known after him split into two. Who is he?
    (a) David Brewster   (b) Wilhelm von Biela
    (c) Heinrich Olbers   (d) Francis Baily

34. The telegraphic code is known after him. Who is he?
    (a) Joseph Henry   (b) Andre Ampere
    (c) Samuel Morse   (d) Jean Fourier

35. Who is renowned for conducting extensive research on the structure of collagen, the commonly occurring protein in the human body?
    (a) G.N.Ramchandran   (b) James Watson
    (c) Frederic Sanger   (d) Jonas Salk

36. Whose mathematical discovery is now used in placing communication satellites around the earth?
    (a) Pierre Laplace   (b) Joseph Lagrange
    (c) Ernest Mach   (d) Arthur C. Clarke

37. The effect known after this scientist's name is used to determine velocities of moving objects whether on earth or in space. Who is he?
    (a) Christian Doppler   (b) C. V. Raman
    (c) Gaspard de Coriolis   (d) Michael Faraday

38. Who proposed the idea that stars generate energy by nuclear fusion?
    (a) Hans Bethe   (b) M.N.Saha
    (c) Albert Einstein   (d) Bertrand Russell

Pathfinders

39. Who forwarded the theory of wave-particle duality, i.e., a particle sometimes behave like a wave, and vice versa?
    (a) Albert Einstein   (b) A. H. Compton
    (c) Louis de Broglie   (d) William Bragg

40. Who coined the term 'Bit' for a unit of information?
    (a) Roger Penrose   (b) Claude E. Shannon
    (c) Charles Babbage   (d) William Shockley

41. Who coined the term 'Information superhighway' for the Internet?
    (a) Al Gore   (b) Bill Gates
    (c) Subeer Bhatia   (d) Tim Berners-Lee

42. Who coined the term 'meme'– any bit of information, whether it is a fact, fad or rumour?
    (a) Richard Dawking   (b) Charles Darwin
    (c) Ren Descartes   (d) William Hamilton

43. Who claimed that Vitamin C can prevent common cold?
    - (a) Linus Pauling
    - (b) Rebe Dubos
    - (c) Paul Muller
    - (d) G. Natta

44. Who postulated the existence of neutrino, an elementary particle that interacts weakly with matter?
    - (a) Wolfgang Pauli
    - (b) Carl D. Anderson
    - (c) James Chadwick
    - (d) Pavel Cherenkov

45. Who maintained that acquired characteristics could be inherited, and violently attacked Gregor Mendel's laws of genetics and other ideas of modern genetics?
    - (a) T. D. Lysenko
    - (b) J. B. S.Haldane
    - (c) Francis Galton
    - (d) George Beadle

46. Who coined the term 'Science'?
    - (a) Francis Bacon
    - (b) Roger Bacon
    - (c) William Whewell
    - (d) Plato

47. Who mathematically deduced that it was impossible to attain the absolute zero temperature, i.e.,–273 degree Celsius?
    - (a) Wilhelm Wien
    - (b) J.J. Thomson
    - (c) Phillip Lenard
    - (d) Hermann Nernst

48. Who proposed the theory of continental drift–
that all continents are drifting like rafts in the sea?
    (a) James Hutton
    (b) George Cuvier
    (c) Alfred Wegener
    (d) Robert Peary

49. Who devised an equipment to measure the charge
on an electron?
    (a) Max Born
    (b) Robert Millikan
    (c) James Chadwick
    (d) C. T. R. Wilson

50. Who coined the term 'collective consciousness'
in psychology?
    (a) Carl Jung
    (b) B. F. Skinner
    (c) Ivan Pavlov
    (d) Sigmund Freud

51. Who forwarded the principle which claims that
there would always remain an uncertainty in
observing the various aspects of an object at
micro level?
    (a) Louis de Broglie
    (b) Werner Heisenberg
    (c) G.W.Leibniz
    (d) Ludwig Boltzmann

52. Who gave some revolutionary concepts about
infinity?
    (a) Kurt Goedel
    (b) Georg Cantor
    (c) G.H.Hardy
    (d) S. Ramanujan

53. Who went deep down into oceans and also high up in the atmosphere to study certain phenomena?
    (a) Jacques Yves Cousteau
    (b) Victor Hess
    (c) Auguste Piccard   (d) Charles Beebe

54. Who gave the Germ Theory of diseases?
    (a) Louis Pasteur   (b) Hugo de Vries
    (c) Claude Bernard   (d) Luigi Galvani

55. Who developed the process to manufacture ammonia on an industrial scale?
    (a) Fritz Haber   (b) Karl Bosch
    (c) Friedrich Bergius   (d) William Perkins

56. Who proposed the theory of anti - particles?
    (a) P.A.M. Dirac   (b) Erwin Schrodinger
    (c) Max Planck   (d) Albert Einstein

57. Who claimed that dreams symbolise the unconscious needs and anxieties of the dreamer?
    (a) Jean Piaget   (b) Plato
    (c) Francis Galton   (d) Sigmund Freud

58. Who gave the equation $E=mc^2$, where E, m and c stand respectively for energy, mass and velocity of light?
    (a) Otto Hahn   (b) Ernest Rutherford
    (c) Niels Bohr   (d) Albert Einstein

59. Who coined the phrase 'survival of the fittest'?
    - (a) Charles Darwin
    - (b) Herbert Spencer
    - (c) Alfred Wallace
    - (d) Eramus Darein

60. Who conducted the famous experiment to prove that nature abhors vacuum?
    - (a) Otto von Guericke
    - (b) John Dalton
    - (c) Joseph Black
    - (d) Evangelista Torricelli

II

ADVENTURERS

Astronauts

61. Which astronaut has become a politician?
    - (a) Frank Borman
    - (b) Thomas Stafford
    - (c) John Glenn
    - (d) Gherman Titov

62. Who was the first man to walk in space?
    - (a) John Glenn
    - (b) Alexei Leonov
    - (c) John Young
    - (d) Alan Shepard

63. Who is the first Asian astronaut to go into space?
    - (a) Rakesh Sharma
    - (b) Ravish Malhotra
    - (c) Sultan Salman Abdel-aziz Al-Saud
    - (d) Pham Taan

64. Who is the oldest man (then 47 years old) to fly in space?
    - (a) John Young
    - (b) Vladimir Shatalov
    - (c) G.T. Beregovoi
    - (d) James Lovell

65. Who were the pilots in the first space shuttle?
    (a) Charles Borman. Guy Gardner, Bryan O
        Conner and John Young
    (b) Robert Crippen and John Young
    (c) Joe Engle and Richard Truly
    (d) Joseph Allen, Vance Brand, William Lenoir
        and Robert Overmyer

66. Who was the first woman in space?
    (a) Sally Ride   (b) Rhea Seddon
    (c) Valentina Tereshkova
    (d) Anna Fisher

67. Who was the first woman astronaut to die during
    a space flight?
    (a) Mary Cleave   (b) Christa McAuliffe
    (c) Rhea Seddon   (d) Judy Resnik

68. Who was the first man to die in space?
    (a) Vladimir Komarov   (b) Yuri Gagarin
    (c) Edward White II   (d) Alexei Yeliseyev

69. Who was the last astronaut to leave the Moon?
    (a) Eugene Cernan   (b) Harrison Schmitt
    (c) Neil Armstrong   (d) Edwin Aldrin

Explorers

70. Who led the first Indian solar eclipse expedition to Jeur in 1898?
    - (a) M.K. Vainu Bappu
    - (b) K. D. Naegamvala
    - (c) A. L. Narayan
    - (d) C. Nagaraja Iyer

71. Who was the leader of the first Indian team that stayed in Antarctica during the winter?
    - (a) H.K. Gupta
    - (b) V.K.Raina
    - (c) S.S.Sharma
    - (d) S.Z.Qasim

72. Who explored central and southern Africa and discovered Victoria Falls, among other things?
    - (a) David Livingstone
    - (b) Alfred Wallace
    - (c) Richard Leakey
    - (d) Henry Norton Stanley

73. Who led the first expedition to Greenland and later proved it to be an island?
    - (a) Robert E. Peary
    - (b) John Milne
    - (c) Gabriel A. Daubree
    - (d) Dicaearchus

74. Who located the site of the North Magnetic Pole?
    - (a) Ronald Amundsen
    - (b) William Gilbert
    - (c) Hans C. Oersted
    - (d) None

75. Who led the first marine expedition to navigate around the earth?
    (a) Marco Polo　　　　　(b) Nicholas of Cusa
    (c) Ptolemy　　　　　　(d) Ferdinand Magellan

76. Who led the first expedition to stay in Antarctica during the winter?
    (a) Leonard Kristensen　(b) James Clark Ross
    (c) Adrien de Gerlache　(d) E. Borchgrevink

77. Who led the scientific expedition that mapped the southern hemisphere of earth, except Antarctica?
    (a) Richard Byrd　　　　(b) Charles Beebe
    (c) James Cook
    (d) Jacques-Yves Cousteau.

78. Who led the Kon-Tiki expedition (crossing the Pacific on a balsa-wood raft) to test a theory?
    (a) Ernest Shackleton　(b)Thor Heyerdahl
    (c) James Hutton　　　　(d) Paul McCready

79. Who is the first Indian to set foot on Antarctica?
    (a) G.S.Sirohi　　　　　(b) S. Z. Qasim
    (c) S.S.Sharma　　　　　(d) S.T.Kulkarni

80. Who is the first man to reach Antarctica?
    (a) Paul Scott　　　　　(b) Thomas Cook
    (c) Fabian Gottlieb Bellingshausen
    (d) Adrian de Gerlache

81. Who is the first man to reach the South Pole?
    - (a) Ronald Amundsen
    - (b) Robert Falcon Scott
    - (c) Francis Drake
    - (d) Ferdinand Magellan

82. Who is the first man to stay alone in Antarctica for five months?
    - (a) Ernest Shackleton
    - (b) Cherry Garrard
    - (c) Richard E. Byrd
    - (d) None

III

CHEMICALS AND ELEMENTS

Chemicals

83. Which chemical compounds may soon be in use as a fuel for driving vehicles?
    - (a) Ethanol
    - (b) Ethene
    - (c) Ethylene
    - (d) Ethane

84. What is the measure of performance of petrol in internal combustion engines?
    - (a) Octave number
    - (b) Octane number
    - (c) Crude oil fraction
    - (d) Kerosene fraction

85. Which material is used in display devices, such as digital watches?
    - (a) Gallium Arsenide
    - (b) Silicon wafer
    - (c) Liquid crystal
    - (d) Quartz

86. What is glass made of?
    (a) Sand, etc
    (b) Calcium, etc
    (c) Boron, etc
    (d) Glycol, etc

87. What is coal gas composed of?
    (a) Methane
    (b) Carbon monoxide
    (c) Hydrogen
    (d) All

88. Which drug is present in Cola drinks?
    (a) Valium
    (b) Cocaine
    (c) Opiate
    (d) Caffeine

89. Which product of living organisms was the first to be made under laboratory conditions?
    (a) Urea
    (b) Glucose
    (c) Fructose
    (d) Amino acid

90. Which fuel produces the maximum heat per gram burnt?
    (a) Gasoline
    (b) Hydrogen
    (c) Oxygen
    (d) Coal

91. Which chemical is added to water supply for the prevention of tooth decay ?
    (a) Fluoride
    (b) Chloride
    (c) Bromide
    (d) Sulphide

92. Which drink has the lowest alcohol content?
    - (a) Beer
    - (b) Vodka
    - (c) Wine
    - (d) Gin

93. How would one know that a chemical is pure?
    - (a) By tasting it
    - (b) By observing its colour
    - (c) By checking its melting point
    - (d) By smelling it

94. What is cement mixed with gravel, bricks or stones called?
    - (a) Lime
    - (b) Chalk
    - (c) Mortar
    - (d) Concrete

95. What is raincoat made of?
    - (a) Polythene
    - (b) Polystyrene
    - (c) Polychlorethene
    - (d) Bitumen

96. Which drug is present in tobacco?
    - (a) Marijuana
    - (b) Heroin
    - (c) Nicotine
    - (d) Cocaine

97. Which is considered to be an anomalous compound?
    - (a) Water
    - (b) Sodium chloride
    - (c) Formic acid
    - (d) Formaldehyde

98. Which chemical is used in a refrigerator for cooling purposes?
    (a) Radon
    (b) Freon
    (c) Sodium
    (d) Fluorine

99. Which chemical causes Minaimata disease?
    (a) DDT
    (b) Cadmium
    (c) Mercury
    (d) Sulphuric acid

Elements

100. Which element can easily form chains?
    (a) Silica
    (b) Carbon
    (c) Hydrogen
    (d) Nitrogen

101. Which is the most abundant element in the earth's crust?
    (a) Oxygen
    (b) Calcium
    (c) Carbon
    (d) Silicon

102. Which element is present in the least amount in a living body?
    (a) Iodine
    (b) Manganese
    (c) Sulphur
    (d) Zinc

103. The addition of one of the following elements to natural rubber makes it less sticky in hot weather and less hard in cold weather. Which is it?
    (a) Phosphorus
    (b) Sulphur
    (c) Carbon
    (d) Silica

104. Which element in radioactive form is used for determining the age of artefacts, relics, bones, etc. of the past?
    (a) Potassium
    (b) Phosphorus
    (c) Sulphur
    (d) Carbon

105. Which disease is caused by the absence of cobalt in minute quantities in the human body?
    (a) Pernicious anemia
    (b) Arthritis
    (c) Leucoderma
    (d) Malta fever

106. What is the most common natural source for sulphur?
    (a) Landslides
    (b) Earthquake-prone region
    (c) Volcanic region
    (d) Agricultural lands

107. Which element is present in the largest amount in a living body?
    (a) Iron
    (b) Sodium
    (c) Phosphorus
    (d) Calcium

108. Which disease is caused by the absence of iodine in minute quantities in human body?
    (a) Insomnia
    (b) Cholera
    (c) Goitre
    (d) Rickets

IV

ACIDS AND GASES

Acids

109. Which acid does soda water contain?
   (a) Carbonic acid
   (b) Sulphuric acid
   (c) Carboxylic acid
   (d) Nitrous acid

110. Antacids are found in medicines that cure this ailment. Which one?
   (a) Headaches
   (b) Pimples
   (c) Stomach aches
   (d) Cataract

111. Which is not a mineral acid?
   (a) Hydrochloric acid
   (b) Sulphuric acid
   (c) Nitric acid
   (d) Glutamic acid

112. Which acid does tomato sauce contain?
   (a) Citric acid
   (b) Acetic acid
   (c) Oelic acid
   (d) Maleic acid

113. What is 'Sulphuric acid' also known as?
    (a) Oleum   (b) Sulphurous acid
    (c) Sulphur oxide   (d) Oil of vitriol

114. Which organism produces formic acid?
    (a) Ants and nettles   (b) Fruits
    (c) Bark of tree   (d) Flowers

115. Proteins are assembled from this acid. What is it?
    (a) Iodic acid   (b) Formic acid
    (c) Nitrous acid   (d) Amino acid

116. Which acid is used as a mild antiseptic eye lotion?
    (a) Boric acid   (b) Carbonic acid
    (c) Hydrochloric acid   (d) Propanoic acid

117. What is the measure of acidity of an acid?
    (a) Iron   (b) pH
    (c) Melting point   (d) Freezing point

118. It is a mixture of concentrated nitric acid and some
    concentrated hydrochloric acid and is used for
    dissolving all metals. What is it?
    (a) Oleum   (b) Aqua regia
    (c) Schiff's reagent   (d) Grignard reagent

119. What is 'Ascorbic acid' also known as?
    (a) Vitamin A   (b) Vitamin C
    (c) Acetic acid   (d) None

120. Which acid do grapes contain?
   - (a) Nitric acid
   - (b) Carboxylic acid
   - (c) Citric acid
   - (c) Iodic acid

Gases

121. What is also known as 'marsh gas' because it is found near marshes?
   - (a) Hydrogen sulphide
   - (b) Sulphur trioxide
   - (c) Sulphur dioxide
   - (d) Methane

122. Which gas is used for killing bacteria?
   - (a) Chlorine
   - (b) Carbon dioxide
   - (c) Nitrogen
   - (d) None

123. In aqualungs, divers mix this gas with oxygen for breathing. Which gas is it?
   - (a) Argon
   - (b) Nitrogen
   - (c) Helium
   - (d) None

124. Which gas is commonly used in balloons and air ships?
   - (a) Hydrogen
   - (b) Helium
   - (c) Carbon dioxide
   - (d) Hydrogen sulphide

125. Which gas is filled in electric bulbs?
   - (a) Oxygen
   - (b) Carbon dioxide
   - (c) Argon
   - (d) Nitrogen

126. Which is the gas released by factories, automobiles, etc. that is most harmful to life?
   (a) Sulphur dioxide   (b) Carbon dioxide
   (c) Nitrogen dioxide   (d) Carbon monoxide

127. A mixture of carbon monoxide and hydrogen, it is a starting material for manufacturing a number of organic compounds. Which gas is it?
   (a) Producer gas   (b) Natural gas
   (c) Synthesis gas   (d) Water gas

128. Which gas is used in those multi-coloured display signs seen at night?
   (a) Xenon   (b) Neon
   (c) Argon   (d) Krypton

129. Which is the most common gas observed in the space between stars?
   (a) Oxygen   (b) Helium
   (c) Methane   (d) Hydrogen

130. What are the major gaseous components of air?
   (a) Nitrogen, Oxygen, Xenon, Carbon dioxide
   (b) Carbon dioxide, Argon, Oxygen, Helium
   (c) Argon, Oxygen, Carbon dioxide, Nitrogen
   (d) Hydrogen, Nitrogen, Oxygen, Carbon dioxide

131. Which gas forms more than 90 per cent of cooking gas?
    (a) Hydrogen   (b) Sulphur dioxide
    (c) Helium   (d) Methane

132. What is solid carbon dioxide also called?
    (a) Solcare   (b) Dry ice
    (c) White carbon   (d) Solid dioxide

133. What is also known as the 'laughing gas'?
    (a) Nitrogen dioxide (b) Nitrous oxide
    (c) Nitrogen monoxide (d) Nitrogen

134. Which gas in liquid form can flow up the wall of a container?
    (a) Nitrogen   (b) Helium
    (c) Hydrogen   (d) Oxygen

V

THE STARRY UNIVERSE

Night Sky

135. On a dark, clear night, how many stars can be seen with the naked eye?
    - (a) 1500
    - (b) 2500
    - (c) 100
    - (d) 250

136. Which star does not move in the sky?
    - (a) Spica
    - (b) Rigel
    - (c) Polaris
    - (d) Castor

137. Which is the brightest quasar known to date?
    - (a) PKS 2000-330
    - (b) 3C-273
    - (c) OQ-172
    - (d) 3C-345

138. Which is the largest constellation?
    - (a) Hydra
    - (b) Dorado
    - (c) Indus
    - (d) Cetus

139. Which is the brightest star?
  - (a) Arcturus
  - (b) Sirius
  - (c) Canopus
  - (d) Antares

140. Which is the smallest constellation?
  - (a) Crux Australis
  - (b) Cepheus
  - (c) Apus
  - (d) Corona Borealis

141. Which star is like our sun?
  - (a) Vega
  - (b) Altair
  - (c) Beta Carinae
  - (d) Tau Ceti

142. Which is the most luminous star?
  - (a) Regulus
  - (b) Spica
  - (c) Neta Carinae
  - (d) Procyon

143. Which planet is also known as the 'morning star'?
  - (a) Mars
  - (b) Jupiter
  - (c) Venus
  - (d) None

144. Which is the finest star cluster in the night sky?
  - (a) Hyades
  - (b) Pleiades
  - (c) Beehive cluster
  - (d) Coma star cluster

145. Which is the largest and brightest globular cluster in the sky?
  - (a) Omega Centauri
  - (b) Messier 53
  - (c) Messier 13
  - (d) 47 Tucanae

146. Which is the most distant object visible to the naked eye?
    (a) Coalsack
    (b) Andromeda galaxy
    (c) Messier 48
    (d) Lagoon nebula

147. Which planet looks reddish in the night sky?
    (a) Jupiter
    (b) Saturn
    (c) Mars
    (d) Mercury

148. Which is the brightest nebula in the sky?
    (a) Orion nebula
    (b) Ring nebula
    (c) Large Cloud of Magellan
    (d) M.42

149. Which comet crushed into Jupiter – creating a spectacular astronomical event in 1994?
    (a) Comet Hyakutake
    (b) Comet Shoemaker-Levy
    (c) Comet Hale-Bobb
    (d) Comet Halley

Big Heavenly Bodies

150. Which heavenly body has been found to have more water than thought of earlier?
    (a) Moon
    (b) Europa
    (c) Phobos
    (d) Icarus

151. Which planet is likely to be colonised in the near future?
    (a) Venus　　　　　　(b) Mercury
    (c) Mars　　　　　　(d) Jupiter

152. Which is the most conspicuous feature on the surface of Mars?
    (a) *Valles Marineris*　(b) *Hells Planita*
    (c) *Olympus Mons*　　(d) *Syrtis Major*

153. Which is the first planet to be discovered in the modern times?
    (a) Mercury　　　　　(b) Pluto
    (c) Saturn　　　　　(d) Uranus

154. Which is the first space probe to reach and study Jupiter?
    (a) *Voyager-I*　　　　(b) *Viking-I*
    (c) *Pioneer-10*　　　(d) *Galileo*

155. Who discovered the ring system of Jupiter?
    (a) G. D. Cassini
    (b) Galileo Galilei
    (c) F.L. Franklin
    (d) *Voyager-I* spacecraft

156. At one time, astronomers thought there was another planet nearer to the sun than Mercury. It was believed to be affecting the path of Mercury. What was that planet called?
    (a) Plato   (b) Ptolemy
    (c) Vulcan   (d) Goya

157. Which is the brightest planet in the sky?
    (a) Jupiter   (b) Venus
    (c) Mercury   (d) Saturn

158. Which is the most conspicuous feature on the surface of Mercury?
    (a) *Hero Rupes*   (b) *Caloris Planita*
    (c) *Planita Borealis*
    (d) *Resolution Rupes*

159. Which planet is renowned for dust storms?
    (a) Earth   (b) Mercury
    (c) Venus   (d) Mars

160. Which planet is next to hell in so far as living conditions are considered?
    (a) Mars   (b) Mercury
    (c) Venus   (d) None

161. What is known as the transit of planet Venus?
    (a) When one sees Venus while one is in transit.
    (b) When Venus crosses the surface of the sun.
    (c) When Venus is observed at the time of solar eclipse.
    (d) When Venus is occulted by another planet.

Small Heavenly Bodies

162. Which is the comet with the shortest periodicity of appearance?
    (a) Encke's comet   (b) Comet Halley
    (c) Lexell's comet   (d) Comet Brooks

163. Where has the largest known meteorite fallen?
    (a) Arizona, U.S.A.   (b) Limerick, Ireland
    (c) Jalandhar, India   (d) Hoba West, Africa

164. Which is the largest crater on the surface of the moon?
    (a) Bailly   (b) Ptolemaeus
    (c) Copernicus   (d) Tycho

165. Which is the brightest crater on the surface of the moon?
    (a) Grimaldi   (b) Plato
    (c) Sarabhai   (d) Aristarchus

166. Which is the first comet known to have hit the sun?
    (a) Comet Encke   (b) 1979 XI
    (c) Comet Donati   (d) Kohoutek's comet.

167. Which is the small heavenly body where volcanic activities have been observed?
    (a) Titan   (b) Vesta
    (c) Io   (d) Moon

168. Which asteroid was the first to be discovered?
    (a) Ceres   (b) Eros
    (c) Habe   (d) Adonis

169. Which is the brightest asteroid?
    (a) Pallas   (b) Vesta
    (c) Juno   (d) Icarus

170. What is the name of the largest crater on Phobos, one of the satellites of Mars?
    (a) Swift   (b) Voltaire
    (c) Stickney   (d) Wendell

171. Where is the heavenly body 'Varuna', named after an Indian deity, located?
    (a) Near Mercury   (b) In an orbit of Moon
    (c) Beyond Neptune   (d) In an orbit of Jupiter

VI

CREATURES – BIG AND SMALL

Novel Creatures

172. Which of the following creatures has the power to grow lost parts?
     - (a) Crab
     - (b) Starfish
     - (c) Squirrel
     - (d) Squid

173. Which is the most primitive living mammal?
     - (a) Seal
     - (b) Duck-billed platypus
     - (c) Weasel
     - (d) Hedgehog

174. Which of the following creatures has the most toxic venom?
     - (a) Kukri snake
     - (b) Krait
     - (c) Scorpion
     - (d) Cobra

175. Which animal is the largest in size?
     - (a) African elephant
     - (b) Blue whale
     - (c) Giraffe
     - (d) Killer whale

176. Which living being has the heaviest brain?
- (a) African elephant
- (b) Killer whale
- (c) Sea cow
- (d) Sperm whale

177. Which animal pretends to be dead when in grave danger?
- (a) Hyena
- (b) Goral
- (c) Crab
- (d) Ibex

178. Which living being's oil is remarkably similar to that extracted from sperm whale?
- (a) Sunflower
- (b) Shark
- (c) Jojoba
- (d) Cod fish

179. Which is the mythical being believed to have become extinct?
- (a) Narwhal
- (b) Nautilus
- (c) Unicorn
- (d) Dodo

180. Which class of living beings' fossils are the least expected to be discovered?
- (a) Ammonites
- (b) Plants
- (c) Gastropods
- (d) Echinoderms

181. Which creature produces the loudest sound?
- (a) Tiger
- (b) Baboon
- (c) Blue whale
- (d) Shark

182. Which of the following creatures possesses the largest eye?
    (a) Frog   (b) Giant squid
    (c) Whale   (d) Giant panda

183. Which living being is a skilled engineer?
    (a) Tailor-bird   (b) Beaver
    (c) Termite   (d) Honeybee

184. Which living being whistles?
    (a) Whale   (b) Dolphin
    (c) Shark   (d) Bat

185. Which of the following living beings has also been found to be a tool-user?
    (a) Sea otter   (b) Gorilla
    (c) Beaver   (d) Spider

186. Which category of creatures contains a type that can fly?
    (a) Cats   (b) Lizards
    (c) Hedgehogs   (d) Rats

187. Which living being has, on an average, the highest life-span?
    (a) Tortoise   (b) Man
    (c) Pelican   (d) Cat

Big Animals

188. Where are zebras found?
    - (a) Africa
    - (b) South America
    - (c) China
    - (d) New Zealand

189. Which of the following animals is on the verge of extinction?
    - (a) Badger
    - (b) Kangaroo
    - (c) Gibbon
    - (d) Great Indian rhinoceros

190. Which has the longest gestation period among mammals?
    - (a) Giant panda
    - (b) Pronghorn
    - (c) Prairie dog
    - (d) Asiatic elephant

191. Which animal can cross-breed with a wolf?
    - (a) Domestic dog
    - (b) Dhole
    - (c) Prairie dog
    - (d) Fox

192. Where are orangutans found?
    - (a) Italy
    - (b) South America
    - (c) North Africa
    - (d) Borneo

193. Which of the following animals is on the verge of extinction?
    - (a) Przewalski's horse
    - (b) Aardvark
    - (c) Python
    - (d) Sea otter

194. Which is the slowest moving mammal?
   - (a) Polar bear
   - (b) Hippopotamus
   - (c) Elephant seal
   - (d) Three-toed sloth

195. Which bovine is most suited to both extreme cold and desert conditions?
   - (a) Bison
   - (b) Gaur
   - (c) Yak
   - (d) Gayal

196. Where are chimpanzees found?
   - (a) Africa
   - (b) South America
   - (c) India
   - (d) Afghanistan

197. Which of the following animals is on the verge of extinction?
   - (a) Tamandua
   - (b) Spider monkey
   - (c) Mountain gorilla
   - (d) Hippopotamus

198. Which mark is used to identify one gorilla from another?
   - (a) Hair
   - (b) Paw
   - (c) Nose-Print
   - (d) Eyebrow

199. Which is the world's largest and rarest lizard?
   - (a) Chameleon
   - (b) Komodo dragon
   - (c) Regal-horned lizard
   - (d) Garden lizard

200. Where are giant anteaters found?
   (a) North America   (b) South Africa
   (c) South America   (d) Japan

201. Which of the following animals is on the verge of extinction?
   (a) Giant panda   (b) Giant anteater
   (c) Pronghorn   (d) Caribou

202. Where are giraffes found?
   (a) North America   (b) Africa
   (c) Canada   (d) Greenland

Small Animals

203. Which animal's teeth are strong enough to fell a tree?
   (a) Squirrel   (b) Beaver
   (c) Chipmunk   (d) Shrew

204. Where are aardvarks found?
   (a) Africa   (b) Australia
   (c) Denmark   (d) Ireland

205. Which rodent is found in remote desert areas, in shifting sand dunes and extreme temperatures?
   (a) Jerboa   (b) Capybara
   (c) Hamster   (d) Murree vole

206. Which animal female curls up round its baby to protect it from any attacking animal?
  - (a) Tortoise
  - (b) Armadillo
  - (c) Pangolin
  - (d) Hedgehog

207 Where are skunks found?
  - (a) North America
  - (b) South America
  - (c) Africa
  - (d) Europe

208. Which is the most successful and rapidly evolving mammal?
  - (a) Hedgehog
  - (b) Panther
  - (c) Horse
  - (d) Mouse

209. Which of the following animals is the fastest burrower?
  - (a) Mole
  - (b) Aardvark
  - (c) Kangroo rat
  - (d) Prairie dog

210 Where are badgers found?
  - (a) Australia
  - (b) South Africa
  - (c) Europe
  - (d) Taiwan

211. Which is the largest rodent in the world?
  - (a) Kangaroo
  - (b) Capybara
  - (c) Rabbit
  - (d) Squirrel

212. Where are koala bears found?
    (a) North America   (b) Australia
    (c) Africa   (d) South America

VII

BIRDS AND TREES

Birds

213. Which bird was once found in abundance but is today an extinct species?
    (a) Flightless cormorant (b) Grey heron
    (c) Passenger pigeon   (d) Kakapo

214. Where is rhea found?
    (a) North America   (b) China
    (c) Ireland   (d) South America

215. Which bird locates its prey by smell?
    (a) Woodpecker   (b) Kiwi
    (c) Crow   (d) Stonechat

216. Which bird mimics the calls and even songs of other birds?
    (a) Koel   (b) Woodpecker
    (c) Eagle   (d) Drongo

217. Which is the fastest swimming bird?
- (a) Gentoo penguin
- (b) Adelie penguin
- (c) Shelduck
- (d) Puffin

218. Where is toucan found?
- (a) China
- (b) Australia
- (c) South America
- (d) England

219. Which of the following birds is on the verge of extinction?
- (a) Monkey-eating eagle
- (b) King penguin
- (c) Dabchick
- (d) Hummingbird

220. Which bird has flippers instead of wings?
- (a) Owl
- (b) Penguin
- (c) Goose
- (d) Albatross

221. Which bird uses its beak as a filter to gather food from water?
- (a) Grey heron
- (b) Ibis
- (c) Flamingo
- (d) Sarus crane

222. Which is the fastest flying bird?
- (a) Albatross
- (b) Sea gull
- (c) Wire-tailed swift
- (d) Spine-tailed swift

223. Which bird keeps its mouth open while flying so that it can catch flying insects?
- (a) Vulture
- (b) Nightjar
- (c) Owl
- (d) Crow

224. Some birds do not catch their own prey. They steal it from another bird. Which bird is it?
- (a) Skua
- (b) Sparrow
- (c) River tern
- (d) Bulbul

225. Which bird holds the record for longest migration?
- (a) Arctic tern
- (b) River tern
- (c) Shearwater
- (d) Barheaded geese

226. Which bird can travel very long distances without flapping its wings?
- (a) Andean condor
- (b) Peregrine falcon
- (c) Coot
- (d) Eagle

227. Which is the heaviest flying bird?
- (a) Ostrich
- (b) Kori bustard
- (c) Vulture
- (d) Condor

228. Which of the following birds is on the verge of extinction?
- (a) Dodo
- (b) Bird of paradise
- (c) California condor
- (d) Bustard

229. Which bird helps in controlling timber pests?
    - (a) Indian grey shrike
    - (b) Woodpecker
    - (c) Tailor-bird
    - (d) Hoopoe

230. Which bird has the biggest egg?
    - (a) Tawny owl
    - (b) Moorhen
    - (c) Ostrich
    - (d) Duck

231. Which bird symbolises Japan but is today on the verge of extinction?
    - (a) Crested ibis
    - (b) Crested skylark
    - (c) Pond heron
    - (d) Black ibis

232. Which of the following birds is threatened with extinction?
    - (a) Black-winged stilt
    - (b) Pied kingfisher
    - (c) Great Indian bustard
    - (d) Fairy bluebird

Trees

233. Which is the biggest plant seed?
    - (a) Walnut
    - (b) Cocoa
    - (c) Coconut
    - (d) Coco-de-mer

234. Which tree was introduced in India by foreigners?
    (a) Pilu   (b) The devil tree
    (c) Coral jasmine   (d) Cashewnut

235. Which is the only species of conifer found in
    Southern India?
    (a) Pine   (b) Cypress
    (c) Juniper   (d) Podocarp

236. Which of the following plants is a carnivore?
    (a) Mimosa   (b) Butterwort
    (c) Hibiscus   (d) Poppy

237. Which is the heaviest plant?
    (a) Giant Sequoia   (b) Pitcher plant
    (c) Banyan tree   (d) Pipal tree

238. Today, India is the main source for this tree. Which
    tree is it?
    (a) Sandal   (b) Sal
    (c) Indian almond   (d) Royal palm

239. Which tree's hard knots are utilised for making
    tobacco pipes?
    (a) Rosewood   (b) Sacred Barna
    (c) Java fig   (d) Teak

240. Which is the most beautiful of all flowering trees in the world?
- (a) Flame of the forest
- (b) Gulmohur
- (c) Flame Amherstia
- (d) Persian lilac

241. Which tree can stand extreme temperatures and is found over a wide range of latitudes?
- (a) Indian screw tree
- (c) Indian poplar
- (c) Karanja
- (d) Jackfruit tree

242. Which is the poisonous tree that can cause death on eating?
- (a) Jangli badam
- (b) Giant milkweed
- (c) Oleander
- (d) Queen's flower

243. Which trees is sacred to the Buddhists?
- (a) Pipal
- (b) Ashoka
- (c) Pagoda tree
- (d) Karanja

244. Which is the largest flower in the world?
- (a) Rafflesia
- (b) Lotus
- (c) Dahlia
- (d) Sunflower

245. Which poisonous plant's name means 'beautiful lady' in Italian ?
- (a) Cowslip
- (b) Cactus
- (c) Belladonna
- (d) Sundew

246. What are cricket bats made of?
   (a) Teak   (b) Rosewood
   (c) Sal   (d) Willow

247. Which flower has been found to contain
    chemicals that can combat cancer?
   (a) Dandelion   (b) Marsh marigold
   (c) Foxglove   (d) Rosy periwinkle

VIII

HUMAN CONCERNS

Human Body

248. Which type of teeth is used for grinding food?
    (a) Molar   (b) Incisor
    (c) Canine   (d) Milk teeth

249. Which bone is of the human arm?
    (a) Sternum   (b) Radius
    (c) Patella   (d) Femur

250. Which of the following is present in stomach?
    (a) Sperm   (b) Dandruff
    (c) Gastric juice   (d) Optic nerve

251. Which is a protein in the human body?
    (a) Collagen   (b) Haemoglobin
    (c) Insulin   (d) All

252. What does gastric juice contain?
   (a) Sucrose
   (b) Bicarbonates
   (c) Hydrochloric acid and pepsin
   (d) Lipids and sucrose

253. Which muscle is of the human thigh?
   (a) *Vastus externus*   (b) Biceps
   (c) Deltoid   (d) Trapezius

254. What is the volume of the brain of an average human being?
   (a) 750 cubic centimeter
   (b) 1500 cubic centimeter
   (c) 4000 cubic centimeter
   (d) 100 cubic centimeter

255. Which gland is present next to the human brain?
   (a) Adrenal   (b) Thyroid
   (c) Pancreas   (d) Pineal

256. Which bone is of the human neck?
   (a) Skull   (b) Sacrum
   (c) Tibia   (d) Atlas

257. What is the normal blood pressure range of human beings?
   (a) 120/80 mm   (b) 110/70 mm
   (c) 140/80 mm   (d) 110/75 mm

258. Where is the fatty, crystalline cholesterol produced in the human body?
   - (a) Pituitary gland
   - (b) Heart
   - (c) Liver
   - (d) Brain

259. Which bone is of the human head?
   - (a) Skull
   - (b) Pelvis
   - (c) Coccyx
   - (d) Scapula

260. Which human organ is least susceptible to harmful radiations?
   - (a) Eyes
   - (b) Heart
   - (c) Brain
   - (d) Lungs

Food and Nutrition

261. Which substance acts like a fuel in driving the body?
   - (a) Minerals
   - (b) Vitamins
   - (c) Carbohydrates
   - (d) Water

262. Beri-beri is due to the lack of a substance. What is it?
   - (a) Vitamin B1
   - (b) Protein
   - (c) Vitamin C
   - (d) Fats

263. What is the unit of measuring the energy requirements of a human body?
    (a) Joule
    (b) Erg
    (c) Kilowatt
    (d) Calorie

264. What kinds of diseases are caused by excess of cholesterol?
    (a) Congenital
    (b) Respiratory
    (c) Cardiovascular
    (d) Cancerous

265. What is destroyed when food is cooked for a long time?
    (a) Essential fatty acids
    (b) Folic acid
    (c) Carbohydrates
    (d) Proteins

266. Which of the following is present in the highest amount in human body?
    (a) Protein
    (b) Fat
    (c) Carbohydrate
    (d) Minerals

267. Intestinal disorders are often caused by the absence of one item in the diet. What is it?
    (a) Fats
    (b) Fibrous material
    (c) Proteins
    (d) Vitamins

268. When a human body starves, muscles waste away to maintain the level of this substance in the body for the functioning of the brain. What is it?
    (a) Glucose
    (b) Folic acid
    (c) Cholesterol
    (d) Vitamin C

269. Which vitamin prevents bleeding of gums?
   - (a) Nicotinamide
   - (b) Thiamine
   - (c) Ascorbic acid
   - (d) Vitamin D

270. What is the simplest form of cooking?
   - (a) Boiling
   - (b) Tenderising
   - (c) Barbecuing
   - (d) Frying

271. Which technique used for preservation of food is most hygienic and harmless to health?
   - (a) Canning
   - (b) Appertisation
   - (c) Irradiation
   - (d) Preservatives

272. Which vitamin prevents night blindness?
   - (a) Vitamin D
   - (b) Vitamin A
   - (c) Riboflavin
   - (d) Folic acid

273. Which country is the biggest consumer of coffee?
   - (a) United States
   - (b) Japan
   - (c) Australia
   - (d) Germany

274. Which country has been able to remove malnutrition?
   - (a) India
   - (b) China
   - (c) Bangladesh
   - (d) Indonesia

275. What enhances the flavour of food containing proteins?
    (a) Baking soda   (b) Caustic soda
    (c) Monosodium glutamate
    (d) Yeast

276. What is the source of the artificial colouring agents for food?
    (a) Fruits   (b) Coal tar
    (c) Lichens   (d) Flowers

Diseases

277. Which disease is caused by a single gene disorder?
    (a) Tay-Sachs disease
    (b) Cystic fibrosis
    (c) Sickle-cell anemia   (d) All

278. Which of the following is responsible for maximun deaths today?
    (a) Cancer   (b) Accidents
    (c) Respiratory disease
    (d) Cardiovascular diseases

279. Which disease that used to kill human beings in millions has today been wiped out?
    (a) Tuberculosis   (b) Smallpox
    (c) Syphilis   (d) Kala-azar

280. Which disease is more common in women than in men?
   (a) Rheumatism   (b) Gastritis
   (c) Coronarythrombosis
   (d) Rheumatoid arthritis

281. Which disease is respiratory in nature?
   (a) Colitis   (b) Ulcer
   (c) Haemorrhage   (d) Emphysema

282. Which contagious disease occurs only during childhood or adolescence?
   (a) Mumps   (b) Smallpox
   (c) Measles   (d) Scarlet fever

283. Which disease occurs from sexual contact?
   (a) Gonorrhoea   (b) Abscess
   (c) Diphtheria   (d) Rabies

284. Which disease is concerned with the eye?
   (a) Glaucoma   (b) Syphilis
   (c) Haemophilia   (d) Pleurisy

285. Which disease concerns the spinal column of man?
   (a) Hypothermia   (b) Cataract
   (c) Cervical spondylosis (d) Hernia

286. What is caused by the blockage of blood vessel by a blood clot?
    (a) Heart failure   (b) Thrombosis
    (c) Arteriosclerosis   (d) Embolism

287. Which disease concerns the bone marrow and tissues that produce blood corpuscles?
    (a) Whooping cough   (b) Leukaemia
    (c) Frost-bite   (d) Gout

288. Which type of food should be avoided as much as possible for maintaining healthy teeth?
    (a) Spicy food   (b) Sugary food
    (c) Salty food   (d) Bitter food

Medicines

289. Why is an antipyretic taken?
    (a) Allay fever
    (b) Reduce blood pressure
    (c) Cure cold   (d) Cure constipation

290. Which disease could be treated using X-rays?
    (a) Cancerous diseases
    (b) Pathological diseases
    (c) Cardiovascular diseases
    (d) Psychological diseases

291. Which birth control method has no side effects?
    (a) Copper-T
    (b) Oral contraceptive
    (c) Intrauterine device
    (d) None

292. What does an analgesic relieve one of?
    (a) Pain   (b) Fever
    (c) Cough   (d) Indigestion

293. What could set right the face disfigured in an accident?
    (a) Medication   (b) Laser beam
    (c) Nutrition   (d) Plastic surgery

294. Which organ is the easiest to transplant from one person to another?
    (a) Kidney   (b) Heart
    (c) Blood   (d) Lung

295. When the kidneys of a person are not working, what treatment is administered?
    (a) Surgical operation on kidney
    (b) Blood transfusion to the body
    (c) Radio therapy
    (d) Dialysis

296. What is a barbiturate?
    (a) Purgative
    (b) Sleeping pill
    (c) Placebo
    (d) Pain-killer

297. Which is the vaccine against tuberculosis?
    (a) Bacille Calmette-Guerin vaccine
    (b) Sabin vaccine
    (c) Salk vaccine
    (d) T.A.B. vaccine

298. What is administered to a patient whose ill health
    is more due to psychological reasons?
    (a) Antibiotics
    (b) Placebos
    (c) Sleeping pills
    (d) Water injections

IX

IMPORTANT LOGIA

Anthropology

299. Where has the large deposit of ape-human fossils been unearthed?
    - (a) Africa
    - (b) India
    - (c) Thailand
    - (d) South Africa

300. Which people are commonly afflicted with sickle-cell anaemia?
    - (a) Negroes
    - (b) Red Indians
    - (c) Europeans
    - (d) Mongolians

301. Which racial group of mankind do the majority of Indians belong to ?
    - (a) Australoid
    - (b) Causasoid
    - (c) Mangoloid
    - (d) Negroid

302. What is 'Lucy'?
   (a) A human-ape fossil   (b) An anthropologist
   (c) A fossil site   (d) None

303. Who are, on average the, heaviest?
   (a) Indians   (b) Europeans
   (c) Eskimos   (d) Australians

304. What does 'Homo sapiens' stand for?
   (a) Wise man   (b) Human being
   (c) Animal group   (d) Tool-maker

305. To which country do the Dogon tribals belong?
   (a) Uganda   (b) Mali
   (c) Mexico   (d) Peru

306. Where was the first fossil of *Ramapithecus,* the ancient man, discovered?
   (a) Africa   (b) China
   (c) Java   (d) India

307. To which state do the Indian Gond tribals belong?
   (a) Uttar Pradesh   (b) Madhya Pradesh
   (c) Bengal   (d) Maharashtra

Geology

308. Which is the most closely studied volcanic eruption?
    - (a) Mauna Loa
    - (b) Mount Etna
    - (c) Mount St. Helena
    - (d) Mount Katmai

309. Which continent was not part of the single super continent 'Panagea'?
    - (a) Eurasia
    - (b) None
    - (c) Indian subcontinent
    - (d) South America

310. Where is the largest and best known geological fault located?
    - (a) California, USA
    - (b) Assam, India
    - (c) Osaka, Japan
    - (d) Mauna Kea, Hawaii

311. Which rocks contain coal?
    - (a) Carboniferous rocks
    - (b) Cambrian rocks
    - (c) Permian rocks
    - (d) Tertiary rocks

312. Which is the instrument used for recording earthquakes?
    - (a) Gravimeter
    - (b) Quake-recorder
    - (c) Seismograph
    - (d) Gravity recorder

313. What is the term that signifies the shape of the earth?
    (a) Geoid   (b) Sphere
    (c) Oblate spheroid   (d) Spheroid

314. Where are mud volcanoes found?
    (a) India   (b) Sri Lanka
    (c) New Zealand   (d) Hawaii

315. Where are 'Nunataks' found?
    (a) Greenland   (b) Australia
    (c) South America   (d) Canada

316. Which is an isthmus (a narrow strip of land join ing two continents)?
    (a) Palk strait   (b) Suez canal
    (c) Bermuda   (d) Bering strait

Archaeology

317. Which item is used for calculating dates of events, etc?
    (a) Tree-rings   (b) Tools
    (c) None   (d) Water

318. Where was the ancient instrument that Greek astronomers used for determining the position of heavenly bodies excavated?
    (a) Sea off Marseille   (b) Sea off Bermuda
    (c) Sea off Port Royal (d) Sea off Andikithira

319. Which item excavated in Indus Valley civilisation is being used to decipher its scripts?
    (a) Seals   (b) Beads
    (c) Stone carvings   (d) Toys

320. Using the satellite Landsat, the origin and path of the mighty and ancient river Saraswati was traced. Where was this river found in India?
    (a) Maharashtra   (b) Kashmir
    (c) Rajasthan   (d) Assam

321. Which archaeological site contained a treasure of gold?
    (a) Franchthi cave   (b) Machu Picchu
    (c) Maltese temples   (d) Tutankhamun tomb

322. Where did research in underwater archaeology start in the world?
    (a) Mediterranean sea (b) Dead sea
    (c) Atlantic ocean   (d) Panama canal

323. What did the Incas, one of the ancient and prosperous civilisations, write numbers, etc. on?
    (a) Beads   (b) Strings
    (c) Wood   (d) Stone

324. Which is the country where 'Nazca lines' (huge figures of animals and birds as seen from the sky) are found?
- (a) Chile
- (b) New Zealand
- (c) Peru
- (d) Tibet

325. Which country is believed to have trade relations with the Indus Valley civilisation?
- (a) Iran
- (b) Iraq
- (c) Libya
- (d) Burma

326. Which Harappan site has a full-fledged dock?
- (a) Kalibangan
- (b) Amri
- (c) Lothal
- (d) Diamadab

327. Which items are an important indicator of the age of the rock in which they are found?
- (a) Fossils
- (b) Crystals
- (c) Cracks
- (d) Dykes

Q. 328. Who is this boyish-looking mathematician? He has created a novel logarithm which speeds up computer calculations.

Q. 329 He is the inventor of the telegraphic code. Who is he?

Q.330 Dressed in traditional Indian clothes and holding his favourite crystal, he is the only Indian scientist to have won the Nobel Prize. Who is he?

Q.331 Who is this bearded, serious-look-ing inventor? He is the inventor of the elevator or lift.

Q.332 Who is this Indian scientist examining a Moon rock? He is the Father of space science in India.

Q.333 This famous US President was also an inventor. Who is he?

Q.334 This Indian is a famous mathematician. Who is he?

Q.335 A French mathematician who also made contributions to cosmology. Who is he?

Q.336 Who is this smiling Indian radio astronomer? He is the brain behind the Giant Metre Wave Radio Telescope installed in India.

Q.337 During his life-time he was the world's leading mathematician and philosopher. Who is he?

Q.338 A Pakistani physicist and Nobel Laureate. Who is he?

Q.339 She is the first Asian woman to go into space aboard the US space shuttle. Who is she?

XI

FRONTIER SCIENCES

Electronics

340. What is a diode used for?
    (a) Converting AC into DC.
    (b) Electrolysis.
    (c) Changing a positive charge into a negative one.
    (d) Generating electricity.

341. Which invention considerably reduced the size of all electronic gadgets?
    (a) Valve   (b) Transistor
    (c) Chip   (d) None

342. What is the main component of a TV ?
    (a) Valve   (b) Cathode ray tube
    (c) Antenna   (d) Screen

343. When you turn the knob of a radio set to catch a station , what do you change?
(a) Radio frequency   (b) Resistance
(c) Voltage   (d) Current

344. What is the diaphragm of a telephone microphone made of?
(a) Silicon   (b) Lead
(c) Carbon   (d) Mica

345. What is used for horizon-to-horizon beaming of signals?
(a) Radio waves   (b) Light
(c) Microwaves   (d) Sound

346. What is a transistor?
(a) Semiconductor   (b) Insulator
(c) Conductor   (d) Superconductor

347. What do coloured strips on resistors stand for?
(a) Their weight   (b) Their resistivity value
(c) Their conductance value
(d) Their nature and quality

348. What is the origin of the word 'Electronics'?
(a) Electrodes   (b) Electret
(c) Electric flux   (d) Electron

349. Which of the following can cause interference in TV reception?
   (a) Supersonic flight   (b) Shuttle launch
   (c) Car   (d) Cycle

Space

350. Which space vehicle fell on the earth like a meteor after staying in space for some time?
   (a) *Skylab*   (b) Spacelab
   (c) *Challenger*
   (d) Satellite Launch Vehicle

351. Which is the first Lunar module that took men to the surface of the moon?
   (a) *Orion*   (b) *Antares*
   (c) *Falcon*   (d) *Eagle*

352. Which is the spacecraft that had two docking ports—the first step towards creation of a permanent space station?
   (a) *Salyut-3*   (b) *Salyut-6*
   (c) *Skylab*   (d) *Apollo-16*

353. Which space shuttle first went into space?
   (a) *Challenger*   (b) *Atlantis*
   (c) *Columbia*   (d) *Enterprise*

354. Which is the aircraft that flew to the edge of space, i.e., above 99 percent of terrestrial atmosphere?
- (a) X-15
- (b) X-20
- (c) T-38
- (d) TU-144

355. Which type of satellites go round the earth at low altitudes?
- (a) Meteorological satellites
- (b) Communication satellites
- (c) Navigation satellites
- (d) Spy satellites

356. Polar regions are ideal for launching manned vehicles into space because of the absence of a phenomenon. What is it?
- (a) Mirages
- (b) Hailstorms
- (c) Van Allen radiation belts
- (d) Solar flares

357. Which is the first man-made object to reach the moon?
- (a) *Sputnik-II*
- (b) *Pioneer-4*
- (c) *Apollo-1*
- (d) *Luna-1*

358. Which is the space shuttle in which Indian-born astronaut Kalpana Chawla went into space for the first time?
- (a) *Columbia*
- (b) *Discovery*
- (c) *Enterprise*
- (d) *Atlantis*

359. Which is the first spacecraft to bring moon rocks to the earth?
    (a) *Luna-1*   (b) *Apollo-8*
    (c) *Luna-16*   (d) *Lunakhod-1*

360. Where did Neil Armstrong set his foot on the moon?
    (a) *Descartes*   (b) *Oceanus Procellarum*
    (c) *Sinus Medii*   (d) *Mare Transquillitatis*

361. Which Indian satellite has performed several diverse tasks?
    (a) *INSAT*   (b) *Aryabhata*
    (c) *Rohini*   (d) *Bhaskara-II*

362. Which space shuttle exploded on its launch?
    (a) *Enterprise*   (b) *Challenger*
    (c) *Columbia*   (d) *Discovery*

363. Which is presently the most remote man-made object in outer space?
    (a) *Pioneer-10*   (b) *Galileo Orbiter*
    (c) *Ulysses*   (d) *Pioneer-ll*

364. What kind of sensors enable a satellite to keep track of missile launches on the earth?
    (a) Ultraviolet sensor (b) Infrared sensor
    (c) X-ray sensor
    (d) Nuclear radiation sensor

365. Which satellite is likely to orbit the earth for the next 50,000 years and will burn up in a spectacular show to announce our presence on the earth?
  (a) *Kalpana-1*   (b) *Sputnik-2000*
  (c) *Kitsat-2*   (d) *K.E.O.*

Oceanography

366. How long is India's coastline?
  (a) About 7,000 km   (b) About 2,000 km
  (c) About 10,000 km (d)   About 15,000 km

367. What is the average depth of oceans?
  (a) 2,610 metres   (b) 3,730 metres
  (c) 4,840 metres   (d) 5,620 metres

368. Which tool has today brought in greater understanding of oceans?
  (a) Super computer   (b) Satellite
  (c) Underwater photography
  (c) Dynamite

369. Which is the most biologically productive, taxonomically diverse and aesthetically important living community in the ocean?
  (a) Coral reef   (b) Undersea volcano
  (c) Island   (d) All

370. Which is the device used for listening in on sea depths?
    (a) Bathysphere   (b) Hydrophone
    (c) Microphone   (d) Bathyscaphe

371. Which marine life is likely to be harvested on a large scale in the near future for consumption as food?
    (a) Krill   (b) Zooplankton
    (c) Whale   (d) Crab

372. What is the modern device used by divers to stay for long periods underwater?
    (a) Snorkel   (b) Diving bell
    (c) Aqualung   (d) Goggles

373. Which gadget is used to ascertain and scan the depths and the floor of oceans?
    (a) Sonar   (b) Radar
    (c) Ladar   (d) Sodar

374. Which is the most polluted sea?
    (a) Arabian sea   (b) Mediterranean sea
    (c) North sea   (d) Weddell sea

375. Where do flat-topped icebergs form?
    (a) Near Greenland   (b) North sea
    (c) Near Antarctica   (d) Nowhere

376. What are oceans rich in?
  (a) Food
  (b) Minerals
  (c) Energy
  (d) All the above

377. What is used for knowing about the past oceans?
  (a) Corals
  (b) Deep sea cores
  (c) Water at various depth
  (d) Shipwrecks

Biochemistry

378. What is known as 'energy molecule' in the living world?
  (a) ATP
  (b) ADP
  (c) TNT
  (d) RNA

379. Which vitamin contains a metal component?
  (a) Vitamin E
  (b) Vitamin A
  (c) Vitamin C
  (d) Vitamin B_{12}

380. Which is the polymer present in abundance on the surface of the earth?
  (a) Wood
  (b) Rubber
  (c) Plastics
  (d) Mud

381. Which type of sugar is found in milk?
  (a) Fructose
  (b) Lactose
  (c) Glucose
  (d) Sucrose

382. Which enzyme do tears contain that kills bacteria?
   (a) Amylase　　　　　(b) Urease
   (c) None　　　　　　(d) Lysozyme

383. Cane juice contains which kind of sugar?
   (a) Maltose　　　　　(b) Glucose
   (c) Sucrose　　　　　(d) Fructose

384. Which is the protein present in human blood?
   (a) Haemoglobin　　　(b) Insulin
   (c) Myosin　　　　　(d) Trypsin

385. Which species of bacteria, if allowed to grow in food, causes poisoning?
   (a) *Saccharomyces cerevisiae*
   (b) *Clostridium botulinum*
   (c) *Streptomyces griseus*
   (d) *Escherichia Coli*

386. When milk turns sour, what is produced for sure?
   (a) Casein　　　　　(b) Lactic acid
   (c) Citric acid　　　(d) Rennin

387. What is the source of peppermint flavour?
   (a) Plant　　　　　(b) Mineral
   (c) Bark of a tree　　(d) Fish

388. What is used as a substitute for sugar?
    (a) Vanilla   (b) Saccharin
    (c) Insulin   (d) Casein

Internet

389. Who runs the Internet?
    (a) Microsoft   (b) Netscape
    (c) National Information Center
    (d) Nobody

390. Which is the language of the web?
    (a) HTML   (b) FORTRAN
    (c) UNIX   (d) JAVA

391. What does this emoticon (emotional icon) stand for}:?
    (a) Kiss   (b) Devil
    (c) Angel   (d) Shock

392. Where are web pages stored?
    (a) Web server   (b) Web browser
    (c) Internet explorer (d) Search engine

393. Which is an outstanding Internet e-mail and news
    program?
    (a) Netshow   (b) Netcaster
    (c) Outlook Express   (d) None

394. What is the formal term for a web address?
- (a) URL
- (b) Website
- (c) Netsite
- (d) FTP

395. What is the rate through which data is transferred between two modems?
- (a) Baud rate
- (b) Bandwidth
- (c) Bps
- (d) Bit

396. Which format is used to compress a PC File?
- (a) Span
- (b) Flame
- (c) Cache
- (d) Zip

397. What is an electronic magazine on the Internet called?
- (a) E-mail
- (b) E-zine
- (c) E-commerce
- (d) All

398. What is the tiny dot that is a part of a picture on the computer screen called?
- (a) Bit
- (b) Frame
- (c) Pixel
- (d) Bar

399. What is an unsolicited e-mail, often making dubious offers or get-rich-quick schemes, called?
- (a) Flame
- (b) Junk e-mail
- (c) Spam e-mail
- (d) Cookie

400. What is a unit of data called?
  (a) Bit
  (b) Node
  (c) Packet
  (d) File

401. Whose job does an e-mail do?
  (a) Newspaper vender
  (b) Postman
  (c) Guardsman
  (d) Milkman

402. What is used for information transfer on the Internet?
  (a) Telephone line
  (b) Radio waves
  (c) Satellites
  (d) All

XII

SCIENCE FICTION

403. Who wrote the classic science fiction *2001: A Space Odyssey?*
     - (a) Ray Bradbury
     - (b) Arthur C.Clarke
     - (c) Stanley Kubrick
     - (d) Douglas Adams

404. Who gave the laws of robotics?
     - (a) Voltaire
     - (b) Stanislaw Lem
     - (c) Karel Capek
     - (d) Isaac Asimov

405. Which is the first science fiction written to popularise especially the concepts of geometry and two-dimensions?
     - (a) *Flatland*
     - (b) *Planiverse*
     - (c) *Dimension A*
     - (d) *Spectrum*

406. Which science fiction film depicted the problems and prospects of an artificially intelligent being?
     - (a) *Men In Black*
     - (b) *The Lost World*
     - (c) *Independence Day*
     - (d) *A.I*

407. Which science fiction mentioned for the first time the possibility of artificial satellites?
    (a) *The Radio Planet*   (b) *The Brick Moon*
    (c) *Rockets to No Where*
    (d) *The Maker of the Moons*

408. Who is the author of the *Martian Chronicles*?
    (a) Edgar Rice Burroughs
    (b) Arthur C. Clarke
    (c) Ray Bradbury
    (d) John W. Campbell

409. Who wrote the novel *Jurassic Park*?
    (a) Michael Crichton   (b) George Lucas
    (c) Stanley Kubrick   (d) Steven Spielberg

410. Who wrote *Frankenstein*, the first science fiction that portrayed the evil consequences of a laboratory-made living being?
    (a) Brian Aldiss   (b) Philip K. Dick
    (c) Mary Shelley   (d) Richard Cowper

411. Which science fiction gave an idea of how computers could be misused today?
    (a) *Star Wars*   (b) *War Games*
    (c) *Prelude to Peril*   (d) *The Iron Dream*

412. Which award-winning science fiction gave a detailed description of a space colony?
   (a) *Cat's Cradle*
   (b) *Rendezvous with Rama*
   (c) *Lost in Space* (d) *Captive Universe*

413. Which is the first computer-generated science fiction movie?
   (a) *Tron* (b) *Star Wars*
   (c) *Alien* (d) *Cocoon*

414. Who writes medical thrillers, of which some have been made into films?
   (a) Isaac Asimov (b) Robin Cook
   (c) Murray Leinster (d) Frank Herbert

415. Which astronomer wrote a science fiction to popularise his ideas about the moon?
   (a) Tycho Brahe (b) Johannes Kepler
   (c) Otto Struve (d) Percival Lowell

416. Which science fiction writer was an expert on rockets?
   (a) James Blish
   (b) Konstantine Tsiolkovsky
   (c) Fritz Leiber (d) Damon Knight

417. Which science fiction writer gave the idea of global satellite communications?
    - (a) Arthur C. Clarke
    - (b) Brian Aldiss
    - (c) Jules Verne
    - (d) H.G. Wells

418. Who wrote *20,000 Leagues Under the Sea*?
    - (a) Jules Verne
    - (b) Jacques Cousteau
    - (c) Poul Anderson
    - (d) H.G. Wells

419. Which science fiction has become a cult today?
    - (a) *The Song of Distant Earth*
    - (b) *Robots and Empire*
    - (c) *The Hitch-hiker's Guide to the Universe*
    - (d) *Dragon's Egg*

420. Which Indian scientist is a science fiction writer as well?
    - (a) C.N.R. Rao
    - (b) J.V. Narlikar
    - (c) E.C.G.Sudarshan
    - (c) Yash Pal

421 Lewis Carroll is the pen-name of the writer of science fiction *Through the Looking Glass*. What was his original name?
    - (a) Charles Lutwidge Dodgson
    - (b) George Ostler
    - (c) Norman Lewis
    - (c) C.O. Sylvester

422. Who wrote the classic *The War of the Worlds?*
    (a) Jermy Campbell   (b) Joseph O'Neill
    (c) H.G. Wells   (d) Nathan Elliot

423. What is the science fictional name of the Internet?
    (a) Cyberspace   (b) World Wide Web
    (c) Net   (d) Netscape

XIII

DATES AND QUOTES

Dates in the History of Science

424. When did the first man–Neil Armstrong–set his foot on the surface of the Moon?
    (a) 1960
    (b) 1969
    (c) 1978
    (d) 1971

425. When was the helical structure of DNA discovered?
    (a) 1960
    (b) 1984
    (c) 1953
    (d) 1904

426. When did Yuri Gagarin circle the earth in a space craft?
    (a) 1967
    (b) 1961
    (c) 1957
    (d) 1975

427. When were the first atom bombs dropped on Hiroshima and Nagasaki?
    (a) 1918   (b) 1940
    (c) 1945   (d) 1942

428. When did Albert Einstein give the General Theory of Relativity?
    (a) 1876   (b) 1900
    (c) 1915   (d) 1960

429. When did the Indus Valley civilisation, one of the oldest in the world, begin?
    (a) 200 BC   (b) 3000 BC
    (c) 10,000 BC   (d) 4000 BC

430. When did Lord Rutherford split the atom?
    (a) 1899   (b) 1945
    (c) 1928   (d) 1911

431. When did the Wright brothers make the maiden flight in a heavier-than-aircraft?
    (a) 1900   (b) 1876
    (c) 1845   (d) 1903

432. When did a huge meteorite fall in Tunguska, Siberia?
    (a) 1901   (b) 1908
    (c) 1877   (d) 1808

433. When did W.K. Roentgen discover X-rays?
    (a) 1900   (b) 1908
    (c) 1895   (d) 1780

434. When did Joseph Lister use carbolic acid as an antiseptic?
    (a) 1790   (b) 1867
    (c) 1678   (d) 1908

435. When did C. V. Raman discover what is known as the 'Raman effect'?
    (a) 1930   (b) 1910
    (c) 1945   (d) 1928

436. When did Robert Goddard launch the first liquid-propelled rocket?
    (a) 1957   (b) 1890
    (c) 1926   (d) 1945

437. When did the Indian mathematician and astronomer Aryabhata give a correct value of π (pi)?
    (a) 412 A.D.   (b) 471 A.D.
    (c) 499 A.D.   (d) 508 A.D.

438. When did Max Planck give his revolutionary theory of quantum physics?
    (a) 1889   (b) 1900
    (c) 1909   (d) 1918

439. When did Henry Ford's Model T– the first car for every man – roll out of the factory?
    (a) 1900   (b) 1904
    (c) 1908   (d) 1912

Quotations

440. Who said 'Genius is one per cent inspiration and ninety nine per cent perspiration'?
    (a) Albert Einstein   (b) Thomas A. Edison
    (c) Isaac Newton   (d) Thomas Jefferson

441. Who said, 'Knowledge is power'?
    (a) Francis Bacon   (b) Albert Einstein
    (c) Aristotle   (d) Euclid

442. Which philosopher of science said, ' It required a very unusual mind to make an analysis of the obvious'?
    (a) Bertrand Russell   (b) Charles Darwin
    (c) A.N. Whitehead   (d) Thomas Lewis

443. Who said, 'Science is nothing but trained and organised commonsense'?
    (a) Peter Medawar   (b) T.H. Huxley
    (c) Archimedes   (d) Julian Huxley

444. Who said, 'Nature is an infinite sphere whose centre is everywhere and whose circumference is nowhere'?
    (a) Salim Ali   (b) Blaise Pascal
    (c) Konrad Lorenz   (d) Roger Bacon

445. Who said, 'Extreme remedies are most appropriate for extreme diseases'?
    (a) Galen   (b) Hippocrates
    (c) William Harvey   (d) Christian Barnard

446. Whose famous and decisive words are 'Yet it does move'?
    (a) Galileo Galilei   (b) Nicolaus Copernicus
    (c) Johannes Kepler   (d) Tycho Brahe

447. Which philosopher said, 'Although this may seem a paradox, all exact science is dominated by the idea of approximation'?
    (a) Karl Popper   (b) Bertrand Russell
    (c) John Ruskin   (d) John Ziman

448. Which playwright once said, 'Science knows only one commandment – contribute to science'?
    (a) Neol Coward   (b) Arthur Miller
    (c) Bertolt Brecht   (d) Oliver Goldsmith

449. Which politician and statesman said, 'The stone age may return on the gleaning wings of fire'?
    (a) Jawahar Lal Nehru (b) Winston Churchill
    (c) Thomas Paine   (d) Joseph Stalin

450. Who said, 'Science is a good piece of furniture for a man to have in an upper chamber provided he has commonsense on the ground floor'?
    (a) Bertrand Russell
    (b) C. P. Snow
    (c) Oliver Wendell Holmes
    (d) Francis Bacon

451. Who gave the following famous statement: 'If I have been able to see farther than others, it was because I stood on the shoulders of giants'?
    (a) C. V. Raman   (b) Thomas Edison
    (c) Isaac Newton   (d) Galileo Galilei

XIV

INDIAN SCIENTISTS AND INSTITUTES

Indian Scientists

452. Who laid the foundation of nuclear science in the country?
     - (a) Raja Ramanna
     - (b) Vikram Sarabhai
     - (c) M.G.K. Menon
     - (d) H.J. Bhabha

453. Who discovered millisecond pulsars?
     - (a) Shrinivas Kulkarni
     - (b) S.Chandrasekhar
     - (c) Shiv Kumar
     - (d) Govind Swarup

454. Who built a chain of scientific laboratories in the country?
     - (a) H.J. Bhabha
     - (b) B. D. Nag Choudhury
     - (c) D. S. Kothari
     - (d) S.S. Bhatnagar

455. Who laid the foundation of chemical industry in the country?
   - (a) S. S. Bhatnagar
   - (b) P.C. Ray
   - (c) T. R. Seshadri
   - (d) C. N. R. Rao

456. Which ancient Indian scientist was a versatile scientist, like Aristotle?
   - (a) Charaka
   - (b) Jivika
   - (c) Varahamihira
   - (d) Kapila

457. Who is the first Indian to win the Kalinga Prize for popularising science?
   - (a) N.K.Sehgal
   - (b) Jagjit Singh
   - (c) J.V.Narlikar
   - (d) Surendra Jha

458. Who laid the foundation of research in statistics in India?
   - (a) C. R. Rao
   - (b) R. A. Fisher
   - (c) J. B. S. Haldane
   - (d) P. C. Mahalanobis

459. Who first gave the basic rules and concept of Yoga?
   - (a) Bhoja
   - (b) Patanjali
   - (c) Dhanvantari
   - (d) Vagbhata

460. Who is considered to have brought green revolution to India?
   - (a) M.S.Swaminathan
   - (b) A. B. Joshi
   - (c) Norman Borlaug
   - (d) D. S. Athwal

461. Who has made major contributions to the 'String theory' of the universe?
    (a) Abhay Ashtekar   (b) Ashoke Sen
    (c) B.V.Sreekantan   (d) Ashok Mitra

462. Who wrote *Rasaratnakara*, a major treatise on alchemy?
    (a) Atreya   (b) Bharadwaja
    (c) Dridhabala   (d) Nagarjuna

463. Whose efforts led to the foundation of the first scientific research institute in India?
    (a) M.N.Roy   (b) M.L.Sirkar
    (c) S.L.Hora   (d) Father Lafont

464. Who is considered to be the inventor of what are known as 'Indian numerals'– the numbers that are used today?
    (a) Sridhara   (b) Aryabhata
    (c) Lagadha   (d) Medhatithi

465. Who was the first Indian to be elected a Fellow of the prestigious Royal Society?
    (a) S.N.Bose   (b) S.Ramanujan
    (c) J.C.Bose   (d) Ardaseer Cursetjee

466. Who discovered the phantom-limb syndrome?
    (a) V.S.Ramachandran
    (b) G.N.Ramachandran
    (c) V.S.Rao   (d) A.S.Paintal

467. 'Science day' is nowadays celebrated on
    February 28 every year in India to mark a well-
    known discovery of this scientist. Who is he?
    (a) J. B. S. Haldane   (b) P. C. Ray
    (c) J. C. Bose   (d) C. V. Raman

468. What discipline of science the Indian technologist
    and president A. P. J. Kalam specialises in?
    (a) Nuclear technology
    (b) Aerospace technology
    (c) Nanotechnology
    (d) Automobile technology

469. Which Indian astronomer discovered an asteroid
    for the first time?
    (a) R. Rajamohan   (b) M. K. V. Bappu
    (c) J. C. Bhlattacharya (d) N. C. Rana

Institutes in India

470. Where is the major cancer research institute in
    India located?
    (a) Chennai   (b) Pondicherry
    (c) Hyderabad   (d) Mumbai

471. Where was science first taught?
    (a) Elphinstone College,Mumbai
    (b) Christian College,Chennai
    (c) Hindu College, Kolkata
    (d) Hindu College, Delhi

472. Where is India's Cyclotron—the particle accelerator machine - installed?
    (a) Mumbai   (b) Kolkata
    (c) Srinagar   (d) Bangalore

473. Which Indian award in science and technology is given by the C.S.I.R?
    (a) Jamnalal Bajaj Award
    (b) Hari Om Ashram Trust Award
    (c) S.S.Bhatnagar Award
    (d) VASVIK Industrial Research Award

474. Which scientific research institute was first established in the country?
    (a) Tata Institute of Fundamental Research
    (b) Indian Association for the Cultivation of Science
    (c) Indian Institute of Science
    (d) National Physical Laboratory

475. Where is the oldest engineering college in India located?
  - (a) Pune
  - (b) Roorkee
  - (c) Bangalore
  - (d) Vellore

476. What was the Indian Agriculture Research Institute known as before the Independence of India?
  - (a) Imperial Agriculture Research Institute
  - (b) British Agriculture Centre
  - (c) East India Institute for Agriculture
  - (d) None

477. Where in India is the fuel for rocket developed and manufactured?
  - (a) Space Applications Centre, Ahmedabad
  - (b) Vikram Sarabhai Space Centre ,Trivandrum
  - (c) SHAR center, Sriharikota
  - (d) National Remote Sensing Agency, Secunderabad

478. Where is the country's biggest optical telescope installed?
  - (a) U.P State Observatory, Naini Tal
  - (b) Vainu Bappu Observatory, Kavalur
  - (c) Kodaikanal Observatory, Kodaikanal
  - (d) Udaipur Solar Observatory, Udaipur

479. Where are cosmic rays being studied under natural conditions?
   (a) Saha Institute of Nuclear Physics, Kolkata
   (b) Institute of Physics, Bhubaneswar
   (c) High Altitude Research Laboratory, Gulmarg
   (d) National Physical Laboratory, New Delhi

480. Where is the major research centre on tuberculosis located in India?
   (a) Mumbai   (b) Hyderabad
   (c) Chennai   (d) Coimbatore

481. Which is the oldest science museum in India?
   (a) Visvesvaraya Industrial and Technological Museum, Bangalore
   (b) National Museum of Natural History, New Delhi
   (c) Birla Industrial and Technological Museum, Kolkata
   (d) National Museum of India, New Delhi

482. Which is the oldest science body in India?
   (a) Indian National Science Academy
   (b) Indian Academy of Science
   (c) National Academy of Science
   (d) Indian Science Congress Association

483. Where is the National Centre for Science Communication located?
   (a) Bangalore   (b) Mumbai
   (c) Kolkata   (d) Hyderabad

484. Where was the first medical college established in India?
   (a) Kolkata   (b) Mumbai
   (c) Chennai   (d) Pune

485. Which organisation produced the first science magazine on the internet?
   (a) Vigyan Prasar   (b) N.D.T.V
   (c) N.C.E.R.T   (d) NISCAIR

486. Which Indian body is exclusively devoted to popularising science among the masses?
   (a) N.C.E.R.T   (b) N.C.S.T.C
   (c) N.R.D.C.   (d) C.S.I.R

487. Which organisation publishes the Indian popular science monthly 'Science Reporter'?
   (a) N.R.D.C.   (b) C.S.I.R
   (c) Nehru Center   (d) I.S.W.A.

488. Where is the Giant Metre wave Radio Telescope (G M R T) installed in India?
   (a) Near Jorhat   (b) Near Pune
   (c) Near Haridwar   (d) Near Ujjain

XV

WOMEN SCIENTISTS

489. What did Rachel Carson write mostly about?
    - (a) Volcanoes
    - (b) Weather
    - (c) Pollution
    - (d) Sea

490. What has Dorothy Hodgkins made important contributions to?
    - (a) X-rays
    - (b) Crystallography
    - (c) Superconductivity
    - (d) Proteins

491. Which woman astronomer discovered six comets?
    - (a) Hypatia
    - (b) Margaret Burbridge
    - (c) Caroline Herschel
    - (d) Christine Wilson

492. What did Mariam Rothschild crusade for?
    - (a) Clean air
    - (b) Animal rights
    - (c) Human rights
    - (d) Forests

493. What has Rosalind Franklin made important contributions to?
   (a) DNA
   (b) Benzene
   (c) Pulsar
   (d) Atom

494. Henrietta S. Leavitt's discovery showed that spiral nebulae are external system millions of light years away. What did she discover?
   (a) Cepheid variables
   (b) Spiral nebulae
   (c) Quasar
   (d) Dark matter

495. What is Margaret Mead renowned for her writings on?
   (a) Zoology
   (b) Meteorology
   (c) Earth science
   (d) Anthropology

496. To what subject did Florence Nightingale, the extraordinary nurse , made scientific contributions?
   (a) Blood transfusion
   (b) Medical statistics
   (d) Genetics
   (d) Anthropology

497. What has the eminent Indian scientist Asima Chatterji contributed to?
   (a) Natural products chemistry
   (b) Polymer chemistry
   (c) Chemical evolution
   (d) Colloid chemistry

498. Whose research concerns how various chemical elements were created in space?
    (a) Kathleen Lonsdale
    (b) Cecila H. Payne-Gaposchkin
    (c) Margaret Burbidge   (d) None of these

499. Which astronomical object's discovery is credited to Jocelyn Bell Burnell?
    (a) Quasar   (b) Black hole
    (c) Pulsar   (d) Infrared star

500. Whose medical text-book *Diseases of Women* published in 1547 became a standard work?
    (a) Trotula   (b) Dorotea Bocchi
    (c) Maria della Donnae
    (d) Anna Morandi Manzolini

XVI

RECORDS

501. Which is the world's largest bay?
    - (a) Walilvis Bay
    - (b) Bay of Bengal
    - (c) Mossel Bay
    - (d) San Francisco Bay

502. Which is the largest fruit?
    - (a) Jack fruit
    - (b) Pineapple
    - (c) Water melon
    - (d) Papaya

503. Which is the longest insect?
    - (a) Silverfish
    - (b) Stick insect
    - (c) Dragon fly
    - (d) Cicada

504. Which is the largest sea?
    - (a) Arabian sea
    - (b) South China sea
    - (c) Red Sea
    - (d) Dead Sea

505. Which is the largest carnivore on land?
    - (a) Malayan sun bear
    - (b) Indian tiger
    - (c) Siberian tiger
    - (d) Kodiak bear

506. What is the hottest temperature recorded on the surface of the earth?
- (a) 48 °C
- (b) 58 °C
- (c) 68 °C
- (d) 78 °C

507. Which is the fastest growing plant?
- (a) Cactus
- (b) Bamboo
- (c) Palm
- (d) Sandalwood

508. Which is the most widely used fibre in the world?
- (a) Nylon
- (b) Wool
- (c) Cotton
- (d) Silk

509. Which is the largest continent?
- (a) Australia
- (b) North America
- (c) Eurasia
- (d) South America

510. Which is the world's oldest tree?
- (a) Bristlecone pine
- (b) Douglas fir
- (c) Mediterranean cypress
- (d) Giant redwood

511. Where is the longest glacier located?
- (a) Greenland
- (b) Australia
- (c) China
- (d) Antarctica

512. Which is the largest flowering plant?
- (a) Chinese wisteria
- (b) Rafflesia
- (c) Sunflower
- (d) Lotus

XVII

MISCELLANY

Science Affects Society

513. 'Whatever happens, we have got
The maximum gun, and they have not'
When did this jingle regarding a latest weapon
become popular during wars between the
Europeans and Africans and Asians?
   (a) The early 19th century
   (b) The late 19th century
   (c) First World War
   (d) Second World War

514. Which is the novel computer invented in India to
cater to Indian needs?
   (a) *Param*   (b) *Simputer*
   (c) *Avishkar*   (d) *Agni*

515. What could be done on a large scale in cities, towns as well as villages to collect the most precious resource on earth – water?
    (a) Groundwater tapping (b) Rainwater harvesting
    (c) Seeding clouds   (d) Building small dams

516. Which technology is likely to come in our lives in a big way and revolutionise various fields, espcially entertainment, architecture, etc?
    (a) Virtual Reality   (b) Computer graphics
    (c) Laser   (d) Fiber optics

517. Which toy-invention became as instant success with children when it was invented?
    (a) Cartesian diver   (b) Binoculars
    (c) Flute   (d) Kaleidoscope

518. Which is the most popular science serial on the Indian television?
    (a) *Kasauti*   (b) *Turning Point*
    (c) *Bharat ki Chhap*   (d) *Imaging Science*

519. Where did the industrial revolution begin?
    (a) Britain   (b) Germany
    (c) France   (d) Belgium

520. Which invention became popular during the life-time of its inventor?
    (a) Television   (b) Computer
    (c) Bicycle   (d) Tyres

Other than Science

521. Who used to deliver 'Christmas lectures' to popularise science among the young?
   - (a) Humphry Davy
   - (b) Michael Faraday
   - (c) William Gilbert
   - (d) James Jeans

522. Which newly discovered scientific phenomenon eventually turned out to be a fraud?
   - (a) Gene jumping
   - (b) Cold fusion
   - (c) Cold superconductivity
   - (d) Hot superconductivity

523. Which astronomer persuaded the Rockefeller Foundation to build one of the largest optical telescopes in the world?
   - (a) John Flamsteed
   - (b) George E. Hale
   - (c) Walter Baade
   - (d) Rudolph Minkowski

524. Which mathematician became blind yet continued his researches in mathematics?
   - (a) Euclid
   - (b) George Cantor
   - (c) Leonhard Euler
   - (d) S. Ramanujan

525. Who is the founder of the cult that claimed that the essence of all things is number?
   - (a) Archimedes
   - (b) Pythagorus
   - (c) Euclid
   - (d) Brahmagupta

526. Which astronomer received the copy of his revolutionary book on the day of his death?
(a) Galileo Galilei   (b) Nicolaus Copernicus
(c) Johannes Kepler   (d) Tycho Brahe

527. Who was killed when he was busy solving a
mathematical problem?
(a) Bhaskara   (b) Archimedes
(c) Euclid   (d) Aristotle

528. Even today a doctor swears by an oath named
after him. Who is he?
(a) Hipparchus   (b) Ptolemy
(c) Charaka   (d) Hippocrates

529. Who was burnt at stake for giving fiery speeches
in support of Copernicus' theory that the sun
and not the earth is at the centre of the universe?
(a) Galileo Galilei   (b) Giordino Bruno
(c) Nicolaus Copernicus
(d) All

General

530. When is the 'National Technology Day' celebrated in India every year?
(a) July 19   (b) May 11
(c) December 1   (d) February 29

531. The Oscar-winning film 'A Beautiful Mind' is based on the life of a Nobel Prize –winning mathematician. Who is he?

(a) John Nash
(b) John von Neumann
(c) Harish Chandra
(d) Norbert Weiner

532. Which space shuttle exploded recently on its return to the earth?

(a) *Atlantis*
(b) *Endeavour*
(c) *Columbia*
(d) *Challenger*

533. Which subject is presently the frontier of scientific research?

(a) Nanotechnology
(b) Cloning
(c) Genome
(d) All

534. What is the name of the Indian space mission to the Moon?

(a) *Trishul-1*
(b) *Nag-3*
(c) *Chandrayan*
(d) *Agni-4*

535. Who visited outer space as a tourist for the first time?

(a) Rick Husband
(b) Mary Cleave
(c) Dennis Tito
(d) Rakesh Sharma

536. Which industry is presently flourishing due to re searches in biotechnology?

(a) Drug
(b) Petroleum
(c) Coal
(d) Food

Q.537 What is it and its specialty?

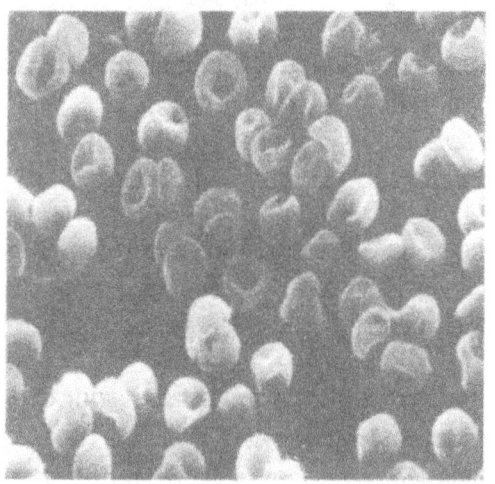

Q.538 What are these petal-like things that are part of our body?

Q.539 This pock - marked object is certainly a heavenly body. Which is it?

Q.540 This is certainly an Indian device. What is its name? What did it do?

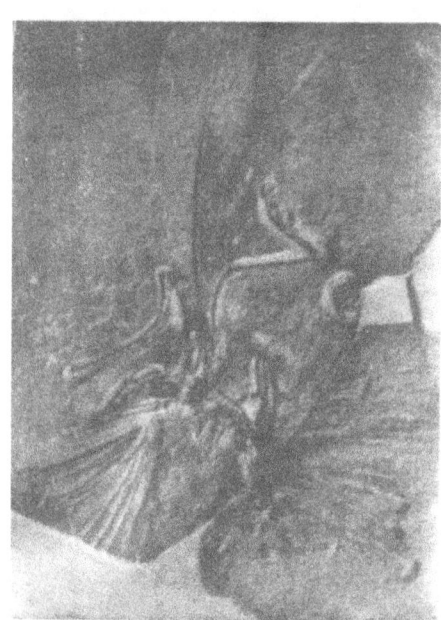

Q.541 This is a fossil of a creature. What is that creature?

Q.542 This contraption is of historic importance. What is it?

116

Q.543 Which is this historical monument? What is its scientific and technological significance?

Q.544 What is so special about this watch?

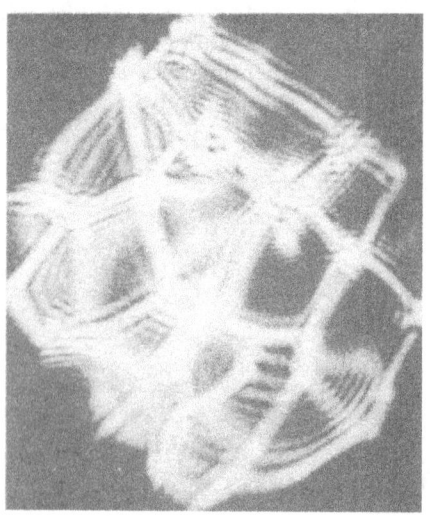

Q.545 A magnified photo of a commonly seen phenomenon. What is it?

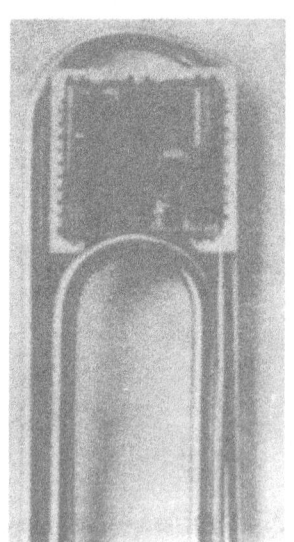

Q.546 What is the object, hardly six millimetres square, sitting on a clip?

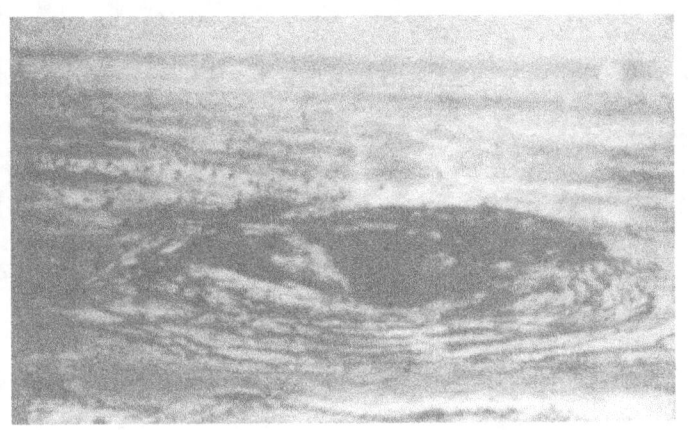

Q.547 What is it? Where is it located? What is its significance?

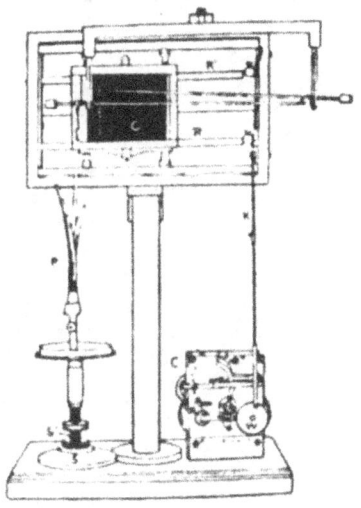

Q.548 This is a sketch of a famous invention. What is it? Who invented it?

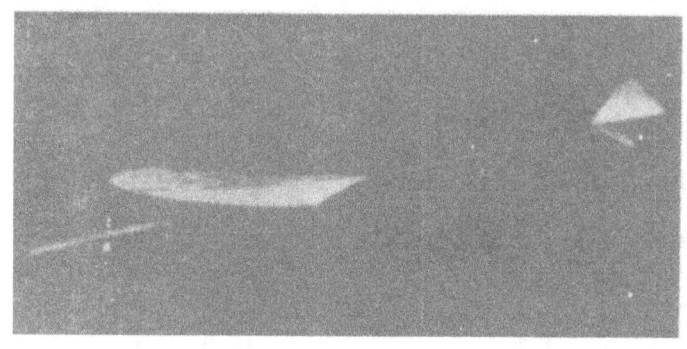

Q.549 A model of something. What is it? Who invented it? When?

Q.550 This photo is neither of a scientist nor of an inventor. It is of an ordinary man. Then, what is special about him?

ANSWERS

1.	(c)	32.	(a)	63.	(d)
2.	(b)	33.	(b)	64.	(c)
3.	(b)	34.	(c)	65.	(b)
4.	(c)	35.	(a)	66.	(c)
5.	(c)	36.	(b)	67.	(d)
6.	(c)	37.	(a)	68.	(a)
7.	(c)	38.	(a)	69.	(a)
8.	(c)	39.	(c)	70.	(b)
9.	(b)	40.	(b)	71.	(c)
10.	(c)	41.	(a)	72.	(a)
11.	(a)	42.	(a)	73.	(a)
12.	(b)	43.	(a)	74.	(a)
13.	(c)	44.	(a)	75.	(d)
14.	(d)	45.	(a)	76.	(c)
15.	(d)	46.	(c)	77.	(c)
16.	(b)	47.	(d)	78.	(b)
17.	(b)	48.	(c)	79.	(a)
18.	(d)	49.	(b)	80.	(c)
19.	(d)	50.	(a)	81.	(a)
20.	(c)	51.	(b)	82.	(c)
21.	(a)	52.	(b)	83.	(a)
22.	(b)	53.	(c)	84.	(b)
23.	(b)	54.	(a)	85.	(c)
24.	(a)	55.	(a)	86.	(a)
25.	(c)	56.	(a)	87.	(d)
26.	(a)	57.	(d)	88.	(d)
27.	(a)	58.	(d)	89.	(a)
28.	(b)	59.	(b)	90.	(b)
29.	(c)	60.	(a)	91.	(a)
30.	(c)	61.	(c)	92.	(a)
31.	(a)	62.	(b)	93.	(a)

94.	(d)	128.	(b)	162.	(a)
95.	(c)	129.	(d)	163.	(d)
96.	(c)	130.	(c)	164.	(a)
97.	(a)	131.	(d)	165.	(d)
98.	(b)	132.	(b)	166.	(b)
99.	(c)	133.	(b)	167.	(c)
100.	(b)	134.	(b)	168.	(a)
101.	(a)	135.	(a)	169.	(b)
102.	(b)	136.	(c)	170.	(c)
103.	(b)	137.	(b)	171.	(c)
104.	(d)	138.	(a)	172.	(b)
105.	(a)	139.	(b)	173.	(b)
106.	(c)	140.	(a)	174.	(b)
107.	(d)	141.	(d)	175.	(b)
108.	(c)	142.	(c)	176.	(d)
109.	(d)	143.	(c)	177.	(a)
110.	(c)	144.	(b)	178.	(c)
111.	(d)	145.	(a)	179.	(c)
112.	(b)	146.	(b)	180.	(d)
113.	(d)	147.	(c)	181.	(c)
114.	(a)	148.	(c)	182.	(b)
115.	(d)	149.	(b)	183.	(b)
116.	(a)	150.	(a)	184.	(b)
117.	(b)	151.	(c)	185.	(a)
118.	(b)	152.	(d)	186.	(b)
119.	(b)	153.	(d)	187.	(a)
120.	(c)	154.	(c)	188.	(a)
121.	(d)	155.	(d)	189.	(d)
122.	(a)	156.	(c)	190.	(d)
123.	(c)	157.	(b)	191.	(a)
124.	(b)	158.	(b)	192.	(d)
125.	(c)	159.	(d)	193.	(a)
126.	(d)	160.	(c)	194.	(d)
127.	(c)	161.	(b)	195.	(c)

196.	(a)	230.	(c)	264.	(c)
197.	(c)	231.	(a)	265.	(b)
198.	(c)	232.	(c)	266.	(a)
199.	(b)	233.	(d)	267.	(b)
200.	(c)	234.	(d)	268.	(a)
201.	(a)	235.	(d)	269.	(c)
202.	(b)	236.	(b)	270.	(c)
203.	(b)	237.	(a)	271.	(c)
204.	(a)	238.	(a)	272.	(b)
205.	(a)	239.	(d)	273.	(a)
206.	(c)	240.	(c)	274.	(b)
207.	(a)	241.	(b)	275.	(c)
208.	(d)	242.	(c)	276.	(b)
209.	(b)	243.	(b)	277.	(d)
210.	(c)	244.	(a)	278.	(d)
211.	(b)	245.	(c)	279.	(b)
212.	(b)	246.	(d)	280.	(d)
213.	(c)	247.	(d)	281.	(d)
214.	(d)	248.	(a)	282.	(c)
215.	(b)	249.	(b)	283.	(a)
216.	(d)	250.	(c)	284.	(a)
217.	(a)	251.	(d)	285.	(c)
218.	(c)	252.	(c)	286.	(b)
219.	(a)	253.	(a)	287.	(b)
220.	(b)	254.	(b)	288.	(b)
221.	(c)	255.	(d)	289.	(a)
222.	(d)	256.	(d)	290.	(a)
223.	(b)	257.	(a)	291.	(d)
224.	(a)	258.	(c)	292.	(a)
225.	(a)	259.	(a)	293.	(d)
226.	(a)	260.	(c)	294.	(c)
227.	(b)	261.	(c)	295.	(d)
228.	(c)	262.	(a)	296.	(b)
229.	(b)	263.	(d)	297.	(a)

298.	(b)	330.	C. V. Raman	354.	(a)
299.	(a)			355.	(d)
300.	(a)	331.	Elisha Otis	356.	(c)
301.	(b)	332.	Vikram Sarabhai	357.	(b)
302.	(a)			358.	(a)
303.	(c)	333.	Thomas Jefferson	359.	(c)
304.	(a)			360.	(d)
305.	(b)	334.	S. Ramanujan	361.	(a)
306.	(d)			362.	(b)
307.	(b)	335.	Pierre Simon Laplace	363.	(a)
308.	(c)			364.	(b)
309.	(b)			365.	(d)
310.	(a)	336.	Govind Swarup	366.	(a)
311.	(a)			367.	(b)
312.	(c)	337.	Bertrand Russell	368.	(a) and (b)
313.	(a)				
314.	(c)	338.	Abdus Salam	369.	(a)
315.	(a)			370.	(b)
316.	(b)	339.	Kalpana Chawla	371.	(a)
317.	(a)			372.	(c)
318.	(d)	340.	(a)	373.	(a)
319.	(a)	341.	(b)	374.	(c)
320.	(c)	342.	(b)	375.	(c)
321.	(d)	343.	(a)	376.	(d)
322.	(a)	344.	(c)	377.	(b)
323.	(b)	345.	(c)	378.	(a)
324.	(c)	346.	(a)	379.	(d)
325.	(a)	347.	(b)	380.	(a)
326.	(c)	348.	(d)	381.	(b)
327.	(a)	349.	(c)	382.	(d)
328.	Narendra Karmarkar	350.	(a)	383.	(c)
		351.	(d)	384.	(a)
329.	Samuel Morse	352.	(b)	385.	(a)
		353.	(d)	386.	(b)

387.	(b)	421.	(a)	455.	(b)
388.	(b)	422.	(c)	456.	(c)
389.	(d)	423.	(a)	457.	(b)
390.	(a)	424.	(b)	458.	(d)
391.	(b)	425.	(c)	459.	(b)
392.	(a)	426.	(b)	460.	(a)
393.	(c)	427.	(c)	461.	(b)
394.	(a)	428.	(c)	462.	(d)
395.	(c)	429.	(b)	463.	(b)
396.	(d)	430.	(d)	464.	(d)
397.	(b)	431.	(d)	465.	(d)
398.	(c)	432.	(b)	466.	(a)
399.	(b)	433.	(c)	467.	(d)
400.	(c)	434.	(b)	468.	(b)
401.	(b)	435.	(d)	469.	(a)
402.	(d)	436.	(c)	470.	(d)
403.	(c)	437.	(c)	471.	(c)
404.	(d)	438.	(b)	472.	(b)
405.	(a)	439.	(c)	473.	(c)
406.	(d)	440.	(b)	474.	(b)
407.	(b)	441.	(a)	475.	(b)
408.	(c)	442.	(c)	476.	(a)
409.	(a)	443.	(b)	477.	(b)
410.	(c)	444.	(b)	478.	(b)
411.	(b)	445.	(b)	479.	(c)
412.	(b)	446.	(a)	480.	(c)
413.	(a)	447.	(b)	481.	(a)
414.	(b)	448.	(c)	482.	(d)
415.	(b)	449.	(b)	483.	(b)
416.	(b)	450.	(c)	484.	(a)
417.	(a)	451.	(c)	485.	(a)
418.	(a)	452.	(d)	486.	(b)
419.	(c)	453.	(a)	487.	(b)
420.	(b)	454.	(d)	488.	(b)

489.	(d)	505.	(d)	521.	(b)
490.	(b)	506.	(b)	522.	(b)
491.	(c)	507.	(b)	523.	(b)
492.	(b)	508.	(c)	524.	(c)
493.	(a)	509.	(c)	525.	(b)
494.	(a)	510.	(a)	526.	(b)
495.	(d)	511.	(d)	527.	(b)
496.	(b)	512.	(a)	528.	(d)
497.	(a)	513.	(b)	529.	(b)
498.	(c)	514.	(b)	530.	(b)
499.	(c)	515.	(b)	531.	(a)
500.	(a)	516.	(a)	532.	(c)
501.	(b)	517.	(d)	533.	(d)
502.	(a)	518.	(b)	534.	(c)
503.	(b)	519.	(a)	535.	(c)
504.	(b)	520.	(c)	536.	(a)

537. *Rohini* – the first satellite launched by Indian rocket, SLV-3.

538. White blood corpuscles.

539. The unseen, other side of the Moon.

540. 'Anuradha', an Indian equipment that studied cosmic rays during a space shuttle flight.

541. Archaeopteryx, an intermediate between reptile and bird.

542. The first radio telescope that detected radio waves coming from the sky.

543. Iron pillar near Qutab Minar, New Delhi. It has been rust-free for several centuries. It indicates Indians were pioneers of 'powder metallurgy'

544. Solar cell driven watch.

545. A twinkling star. Turbulence in the air caused scattering of light.

546. A single chip – the brain of a computer.

547. The crater in Pokharan, Rajasthan, created by the first nuclear device exploded by India in 1974.
548. Crescograph to measure the pulse beats of plants invented by J. C. Bose.
549. The firm model glider invented by George Cayley in 1804.
550. Ali Maow Maali of Somalia – the last recorded victim of smallpox.

SCORE YOURSELF

Count the correct answers you have given and mark yourself as follows:

Average: if 350-399 answers are correct

Good: if 400-449 answers are correct

Excellent: if 450-499 answers are correct

And if you score more than 500 correct

you are a **SUPER GENIUS** in science!